INVASION

OF THE IQ SNATCHERS

ARTHUR SLADE'S CANADIAN CHILLS #3

INVASION
OF THE IQ SNATCHERS

ARTHUR SLADE

COTEAU BOOKS FOR KIDS

Edited by Barbara Sapergia.
Cover images: "A young boy holding a ceramic cup, Maine USA" by Jose Azel/ Getty Images, "Ant (Formicidae), close-up," by Spike Mafford/Getty Images,and photo of the Bastion by David Hill-Turner/Nanaimo Museum.
Cover and book design, and cover photo montage by Duncan Campbell.
Printed and bound in Canada by Marquis Book Printing.

National Library of Canada Cataloguing in Publication Data

Slade, Arthur G. (Arthur Gregory)
    Invasion of the IQ snatchers / Arthur Slade.

(Arthur Slade's Canadian chills #3)
ISBN 978-1-55050-361-6

I. Title. II. Series: Slade, Arthur G. (Arthur Gregory). Canadian Chills ; #3

PS8587.L343I58 2007   jC813'.54   C2007-901254-X

10 9 8 7 6 5 4 3 2 1

COTEAU BOOKS
2517 Victoria Ave
Regina, Saskatchewan
Canada S4P 0T2

available in Canada and the US from:
Fitzhenry & Whiteside
195 Allstate Parkway
Markham, Ontario
Canada L3R 4T8

The publisher gratefully acknowledges the financial assistance of the Saskatchewan Arts Board, the Canada Council for the Arts, the Government of Canada through the Book Publishing Industry Development Program (BPIDP), the Association for the Export of Canadian Books and the City of Regina Arts Commission, for its publishing program.

*This book is dedicated to
all the friendly* BHM's, ETs,
and Nanaimoites on the island.

CHAPTER ONE

DIRTY ROTTEN HAIRY THIEF!

A long, hairy arm reached through my open window and pounded around the top of my desk.

I stared, eyes wide, sitting in my chair. The first thing I thought was: *that man has the hairiest arms in the world.* Then I saw that the fingernails at the end of spindly, hairy fingers were painted with pink nail polish. So I thought: *that woman has the hairiest arms in the world.*

The hand knocked over my jar of pencils, bumped my Einstein bobble-head statue, and flicked the latest copy of *Science Weekly* to the floor. Finally, it found the plate of untouched Nanaimo bars, picked them up and pulled them toward the window.

I grabbed the other side of the plate and began a heroic tug-of-war. The bars were so sticky they didn't slide around.

"Hey!" I yelled.

"Hey!" Archimedes shouted. He flapped his parrot wings and flew to the top of his cage. "Hey!"

I was too busy holding the plate with a steely grip to talk back to Archimedes. "Not my Nanaimo bars! They were a gift from an unknown admirer."

The hairy woman's arm (I assumed there was a body attached to it, but scientists aren't supposed to jump to conclusions) pulled hard. My chair lurched forward on its wheels and I slammed into the desk, smacking my knees. But I still clenched the plate.

"Ugh!" came a grunting from outside the window. "Uuuurgh uggh!!"

She gave another yank and pulled me up onto the desk.

"You can't have them!" I held on with all my strength. "They're my favourite food group!"

I do know that Nanaimo bars aren't a food group all by themselves. That's just a joke that we use in Nanaimo to express how good they taste and how important they are to the city.

The arm yanked again and the plate came free. Before I could move, the arm, the plate and the Nanaimo bars disappeared out the window.

"No one steals from Gordon Whillickers!" I shouted. Which I immediately knew was a false statement, since someone had once swiped my calculator. "Not without a fight at least."

"Fight! Fight!" Archimedes echoed. "Fight!"

With his words echoing in my ears, I dived through the window, expecting to tangle with an extremely hairy woman. Instead, I heard only the snapping of branches at the far end of our leafy yard. Dad does botany as a hobby, and has grown every sort of shrub, bush, plant and tree he could jam into our soil. I glimpsed a rather large foot that looked hairy, or maybe she was wearing mukluks, then the dastardly thief plopped over the slat fence and out of sight.

I ran, dodging bushes and smashing through the rhododendrons and roses. I dashed up to our fence and scrambled to the top. From that height, I glared down into the Reids' yard. No sign of the thief. Not even a smidgen of movement.

I jumped over and stalked around. The further I got from our house, the more my brain began to analyze the situation. These are the three conclusions I came up with: a) I didn't know who the thief was. b) If she stole willingly, she might also be willing to break other laws. c) She could be dangerous.

But the legendary Whillickers stubbornness rose up and took control of my thoughts. No. They were *my*

Nanaimo bars, someone had left them on a plate at the front door with *my* name on them and I hadn't even had a bite yet. Maybe they were the most delicious batch ever made. I'd planned on rewarding myself after I was done writing a paper about space elevators. Now they were just a memory.

The Reids' dog, Bruiser, was in his doghouse. Why hadn't he barked? I got on my knees and looked in. "Come on boy!" All I could see were his two glowing eyes. "What are you doing in there? Shouldn't you be chasing thieves?"

He was a big dog, but in the shadows he looked even bigger – as though he were filling up the whole doghouse. I peered. He blinked two yellowish eyes.

"Bruiser?"

Maybe it wasn't Bruiser. He certainly wasn't acting like himself.

"Bruiser?" I took a step back. Another.

A nose poked out of the doghouse, came a little further and sniffed. Then a head slowly emerged.

It was Bruiser. He looked frightened, a look I'd never seen on his German shepherd face. He glanced left and right, then lowered himself to the ground as though coming out into the open had sucked up all his energy.

"It's okay, boy," I whispered. "We're safe."

I patted his back. He was shivering like it was -40 degrees Celsius. What could scare him?

I was much more careful as I searched around the Reids' yard for clues. There wasn't even a sign of the Nanaimo bars.

I went to the fence at the back of their yard. Had the thief climbed out here? I couldn't tell. It was as though she had completely and utterly vanished into the pine-scented British Columbia air.

CHAPTER TWO

A BIRD'S-EYE VIEW OF THE FACTS

Archimedes was waiting for me in my office. Of course, he had no choice, being locked in his cage. "Who won? Who won?" he asked, flapping his grey wings. "Tell Archie now." His tail feathers were such a bright red, they seemed to flash.

"Do you see me holding a plateful of Nanaimo bars?"

He blinked his parrot eyes. "No bars. No bars. Gordy is a loser! Loser!"

Now, most people would think having a talking Congo African Grey parrot would be an absolutely excellent thing, but they haven't met Archimedes. He is loud, rude, and about as annoying as ten little brothers. Thanks, Mom and Dad! They picked him up on one of their many trips to Africa. Why not just bring back a tiny hyena? It'd be friendlier.

It was my fault he was so smart. I fed him a special supplement of vitamins and minerals, along with his usual almonds, cheese and leafy greens. But I also used ornithopetic IQ-raising songs on my MP3 player (it's hard to get headphones on a parrot). Oh, and I let him play my Gameboy. He can kick my gluteus maximus anytime. In fact I won twenty dollars when he beat Bill, our neighbour's son, at Donkey Kong.

"Gordy is a loser!" Archimedes sang. "Loser to the max!"

"You're not helping, Archie. This is serious, someone stole from me. From us! I was going to share a Nanaimo bar with you."

His parrot eyes widened. "You catch the thief! Now!"

"That's exactly what I'm going to do. It shouldn't be hard to find her, there can't be that many women with arms that hairy in Nanaimo, can there?"

Archimedes was silent.

"Now, a brilliant scientist, such as Newton, or Carl Sagan, would look at the facts. Fact number 1: There was a plate of Nanaimo bars. Fact number 2: They're gone. Fact number 3: Someone with hairy arms stole them."

"Fact number 4: You talk to yourself all the time," a voice said from outside.

I leaned my head out the window and looked down. It was Sophia, my annoying friend, standing there, her sandy blond hair held out of her eyes with a barrette. She was clad in her typical outdoor outfit, blue T-shirt, blue-jean shorts, grey hiking socks and hiking boots. She said her feet never got cold.

"I don't talk to myself all the time," I said.

"Do so!" Archimedes sang. "Archie hears you talk. All the time."

"I bet you even talk to yourself in your sleep," Sophia said.

"Gordy talks all night! Keeps Archie up!"

They were ganging up on me. "This isn't getting my Nanaimo bars back!"

"Nanaimo bars? Did you get some too?" Sophia asked.

"Yes."

"I had a plateful turn up on my doorstep this morning. It was weird – someone rang the doorbell, then ran away. I wished they'd stuck around. I would have told them I don't really like Nanaimo bars, politely, of course."

It was one of the oddest things about Sophia, not liking Nanaimo bars. I'm surprised the town hadn't conglomerated into a mob and chased her off Vancouver Island. Or at least down to Victoria.

"They had a note on them," she continued. "It said, *'To the smartest girl in Nanaimo.'* So obviously whoever left them knew what they were talking about."

"My bars had a note too," I said. "*'To the smartest boy in Nanaimo.'* And my bars were stolen." I climbed out the window and explained to her everything that had happened so far.

"It's obviously a woman with callused feet," Sophia said.

"What? How can you tell that?"

She pointed. "See her footprints?"

I looked down. There was one clear footprint in the garden soil below my window.

"She was in bare feet," Sophia said.

"I can see that. I'm not blind or otherwise optically impaired. She also must have weighed quite a bit, judging by how deep the print is."

"That's what happens when you eat too many Nanaimo bars," Sophia said. "And she certainly has gunboats for feet. All we have to do is find a large woman with hairy arms and big feet."

"That could be any female teacher in Nanaimo," I said.

She gave me a nasty look.

"I'm kidding. Really, I was just trying to be funny. I forgot your mom is a teacher."

"You stick to science. I'll do any interviews that we need to solve our case."

"I don't need your help!" I said. "I can solve this on my own."

"Well, two heads are better than one. And I was robbed too, remember. My Nanaimo bars were gone. I assumed my brother took them, but now it seems more likely that they were swooshed away by the hairy-armed bandit."

"Fine! Just don't get in my way and don't get all bossy."

"I'll only get bossy if you need it." She rubbed her chin. "Don't you find it odd that all these Nanaimo bars are being handed out?"

"Yes, come to think of it," I said. "Maybe it's some kind of promotion. I wonder if it's just our block or if it's the whole city."

"Why don't we look?" she asked. She began walking towards the front yard.

"You're not going to walk, are you?" I asked.

"That's why I've got feet."

"Well, go ahead, I won't walk. There are too many houses. I've got a better idea."

"Which is?" she asked.

"Oh, you'll find out. Follow me into my office." I climbed in the window first, and when Sophia was in I let her sit in my chair. I turned on my laptop and opened my cupboard, getting a special, tiny helmet out of it.

Then I let Archimedes out of his cage. He flew onto the back of the chair. "Archie will fly excellent!" I carefully attached the helmet to his head and the Velcro straps held it tight. Then I clicked on the switch to the birdcam.

"We're gonna get a bird's-eye view," I said.

"Ho! Ha! You're hilarious! But I must say this is extremely clever of you."

"That's me, extremely clever to the extreme. Archie is going to do all the legwork for us...wingwork, that is." I pressed the button on the computer and a view of my face appeared on the screen. Then we were treated to the sight of scattering cheese bits and green leaves as Archimedes filled himself up before the flight. He took two slurping gulps of water. "Are you ready?" I asked.

He opened up his black beak and stuck out his tongue, which was his way of saying he was ready. He looked a little like a World War I pilot. "Contact!" he said, spreading his red tail feathers. "Contact!" He made a BRRRRRRRZZT sound. He sometimes thought he was a biplane. I rubbed his beak.

"Okay, take off."

"Banzai!" he shouted, then he spread his wings and flew low over the desk, making a few papers flutter. He swooped out the window and into the backyard.

Archie's a good talker, but not a great flyer. He skimmed above the birdbath, nearly knocked his helmet off on the pine tree's branches, then flapped his way above the street.

There he went from door to door, sometimes landing on windowsills. He had to go two blocks before he saw a plate of Nanaimo bars at the front door of a house. He swooped down and we got a view of it, then he flapped on. Most houses had Nanaimo bars in front of them with notes like *"To the prettiest girl in Nanaimo"* or *"To the greatest dad in Nanaimo"* or an odd one that said *"To the clowniest mom in Nanaimo."*

"That's the Schellinck home. Mrs. Schellinck is a professional clown."

"I would have figured that out."

I had the feeling that soon we would find out who was delivering all of these bars. Maybe it was a mayoral campaign. There had to be a giant factory somewhere, or thousands of grandmothers working day and night, to make so many Nanaimo bars. Archie swooped past several more doorsteps dotted with plates of Nanaimo bars. But a block further away, there were no more bars. They had all been stolen, taken inside, or perhaps they hadn't been delivered yet.

"Higher!" I barked into the walkie-talkie. Archimedes flew several stories above the rooftops, to give us a traffic helicopter view. He turned his head and I saw ferries at the dock. He turned again and I glimpsed a mess of buildings towards the downtown. I thought I could even see the Bastion tower. Then suddenly everything flipped upside down.

"Don't fly upside down!" I shouted. Archimedes immediately flipped right side up. He looked down at the street and a distant flash of silver flickered on the screen.

"Follow that flash," I commanded.

Archimedes dived down towards it, but the flash appeared and disappeared. I couldn't get a fix on what it was. He swooped past the rooftops and zeroed in on the object. It was zipping along the sidewalk faster than an unmanned skateboard. I squinted at the screen.

Archie hovered above the strangest sight I'd ever seen. It was a pan full of Nanaimo bars, shooting along the sidewalk all on its own.

CHAPTER THREE

OUT OF THE NANAIMO PAN...

"Closer!" I commanded. Archimedes hovered above the zooming pan. "Closer."

He landed on it. The pan continued zipping along even when he spread out his wings and dragged one foot on the ground. Archie walked over to the edge and bent over, looking underneath.

About twenty beady eyes glared out at him. Dark eyes, attached to round metallic heads which were attached to abdomens with six legs.

"Ants!" Sophia said.

"Robot ants," I corrected. They were working their robot butts off, each carrying a share of the load of the pan. Even Archie's extra weight didn't seem to bother them.

Actually, I should point out that ants don't actually have butts. That section of their body is, of course, called an abdomen.

"Keep riding it," I said.

"10-4! 10-4!" Archie responded. The pan scooted down the sidewalk, then took a sharp turn, nearly dumping Archie. It came to a sudden stop in font of a house. Archie watched as the ants lowered it down. One ant scurried over to the house, zipped up the frame, and rang the doorbell. Then it hustled back down and joined its fellow robot ants. They stood silently for a moment, antennae waggling, then, as though they'd received a message from the sky, all of them charged to the edge of the sidewalk. One ant's mandible began to spin and it drilled its way into the earth, dirt flying out of the hole. Within a moment it was gone and all its fellow ants followed.

The door opened.

"Get off those Nanaimo bars, you dirty bird!" a woman screeched. A broom appeared on the screen, swooping towards Archie, who took to the air in a flash.

"Come home, Archie," I said. "Home!"

Soon we were treated to a bird's-eye view of a woman shaking her broom, looking like Queen Kong in curlers. Archie fled towards our house. I turned off the camera.

"Robot ants," I said. "Even the CIA or NASA don't have robot ants yet."

"Do you thinks it's the Russians? The Germans? The Nunavutians?"

"Who?"

"The people who live in Nunavut. No one would ever expect them."

I shook my head. "I don't know who it is. But the question is, what do they want? And why? Are they bribing the whole town?"

"And why would the hairy-armed woman steal the bars?"

That was another good question. I wish I knew what was in the bars. Was it the original secret recipe? Or was it something else?

"This is big," I said. "It's going to require a lot of deep thinking."

"Fine, I'll help you," Sophia said.

"That's not what I was saying."

"No, no." She put up her hands. "Don't beg. I said I'd help."

"Well, I do need a lackey, so to speak. A grunt."

"Charming, Gordon. Now tell me, wise guy, how do we track down whoever created those ants?"

"Ha! The answer is simple!" I put my finger in the air, hoping that the answer would pop into my head. It didn't. In fact a big fat nothing popped into my skull. "Well, it's uh…"

"Since the ants went underground, we can't follow them," Sophia said. "But maybe we're looking down the wrong hole, so to speak. If we find out who's stealing the Nanaimo bars, then we'll likely find out who's making them. And while we're at it, maybe we should get a plate of those bars and do a few experiments on them."

"That's exactly what I was thinking." She was out-thinking me. That wouldn't do. I had to out-think her. "We'll have to get that plate from Mrs. Schellinck."

"It's like you're reading my mind," Sophia said.

"We'll go over there and tell her we're collecting bottles, then sneak into her house, set off the smoke alarm by burning some toast and while she runs out we'll grab the bars."

"That might work," Sophia said. "But why don't we just ask for one? I'm sure she'd give us each a piece."

"Uh, we can try that," I said.

Archimedes swept in squawking and fluttering and crash-landing on my desk. I removed the helmet and patted his head. "Good work."

"Archie knows. Archie is the best," he answered. One thing about Archie, he isn't humble.

I carried him to his cage and gave him an extra treat,

candied almonds. He went to work on it right away, pausing only to whistle.

Sophia and I slipped out of the room, went down the hall and stopped at the front door. I paused, wondering if there were any scientific instruments I should be bringing with me. Little did I know, the thing I needed most was a Weirdness Detector, because things were about to get extremely and utterly weird.

CHAPTER FOUR

A STRANGE SERIES OF WEIRD EVENTS

"Oh, Gordon," my mom called. "Gordon Liam Nicholas Whillickers, my favourite son."

"I'm your only son, Mom," I said.

My mother, Millicent Whillickers, was vacuuming. I did a double take. She wasn't big into vacuuming (it was Dad's job) and the last time I'd seen her do it was before my sixth birthday. Maybe she'd spilled some sugar. Her hair was also in curlers. I'd never seen her with curlers.

"Did you do your homework?" she asked.

"It's summer, Mom. I don't have homework."

She clicked off the vacuum. "Summer? Already?" She scratched at one of her curlers.

Worry forced my brow to furrow. "It's still summer, Mom. Are you all right?"

She laughed, a dry crackly noise. "Of course, I'm peachy and keen. I knew it was summer. Did you make your bed and brush your teeth?"

This was getting a little embarrassing. "Yes, Mom."

"Did you wash behind your ears?"

"Uh, I think so."

"Good boy. You're my favourite son," she said. "What time is it?"

"It's two p.m."

She dropped the vacuum as if it had given her a 60-volt shock. "Two p.m.! Coronation Street is on! I must watch it! Now! I never miss it!"

She dashed to the TV room, curlers bouncing. I gave my head a good hard shake. Nothing seemed to be rattling. "That was really weird."

"Uh, did, like, your mom bump her head this morning?"

"She must have," I said. "She never vacuums and never watches TV. Especially not soaps like Coronation Street. Maybe she forgot to drink her coffee. Sometimes that'll make her go all loopy."

We left the house and I was still shaking my head. "Or maybe it's a sugar high. I bet she had a chocolate bar or something."

Anyway, we had more important mysteries to figure out than a parent malfunction. We walked up to the Schellinck home. When we rang the doorbell it made a clown-like laughing sound – Mrs. Schellinck took her job seriously. But she obviously didn't take her doorbell seriously because she didn't come to the door. We made the doorbell laugh several more times.

"I know she's in there," Sophia said. "I can hear the TV."

"Yeah. Me too." It was amazingly loud.

A British doctor on Coronation Street was saying, "You've only got six days to live. Unless we can get you a brain, lung and heart donor right away. Sorry to give you this beastly awful news."

Sophia crossed her arms. "Well, I'm a little worried about Mrs. Schellinck. Do you think she's okay? Maybe she was practicing on her unicycle and fell off in her living room."

"Lets take a look around back."

We tiptoed across the perfectly cut lawn to the back of the house and peeked in the patio window. Mrs. Schellinck was in her La-z-Boy chair, feet up, curlers on, watching Coronation Street. She was slowly eating the Nanaimo bars.

"I'm going to knock," I said.

Sophia nodded. I knocked and Mrs. Schellinck didn't budge, other than to bring another Nanaimo bar to her mouth. I slid the door slightly open and whispered, "Mrs. Schellinck. Mrs. Schellinck." She ignored me.

Finally, Sophia and I walked in. The TV was blaring at about 100 decibels. Someone on Coronation Street shouted in a British accent, "Oh my, there's been a horrible lift-and-lorry accident."

"Guess we found your donor, blinking bad luck for them," the doctor said. "Righto, let's get these lungs, heart and brain into you."

I turned the corner of her massive chair. Mrs. Schellinck was staring so hard at the TV that her eyes were dull and hypnotized. She didn't blink. I waved my hand in front of her. She still didn't blink.

"Mrs. Schellinck! Mrs. Schellinck!" I practically shouted.

"This is very odd," Sophia said. "Do you think she's in a catatonic state?"

"Definitely! In fact I'd say ultra-catatonic." She had a clown horn next to her chair, I honked it and she didn't even shudder.

I looked at the TV. A woman in curlers was dabbing at her eyes with a handkerchief, whispering, "What a horrible way to go." Oddly enough, with the curlers on she reminded me of Mom. Before I could think further about this, the credits to Coronation Street were coming on and a voice said, "Be sure to tune in the same time tomorrow. The show that'll excite your brain patterns. Coronation Street."

Excite your brain patterns? What did that mean? Then a commercial for condos came on.

Mrs. Schellinck blinked. "Gordon! Sophia! What a surprise."

"We thought you were in catatonic state."

She grinned. "Me? No! Never. I just had a catnap. What are you doing here?"

"Uh," I said, searching my brilliant scientist brain for an excuse. "We uh…"

"Came because you invited us for Nanaimo bars." Sophia reached for the plate.

Mrs. Schellinck snatched the plate away and hid it on the other side of the chair. "No. Not those ones. I'm afraid I don't have any. You'll have to go away." She shot up suddenly. "I have vacuuming to do. Vacuuming! You'll have to come back another time."

She shooed us outside and a moment later her vacuum roared to life. We started walking back.

"What was that all about?" I asked. "She *was* in some kind of odd state. Vacuuming! Curlers! Coronation Street! I wish we could have gotten one of those Nanaimo bars."

"We did," Sophia said. She opened her hand and a familiar chocolate-and-yellow bar sat in her palm. "I palmed it, so to speak. While she was watching her soap."

CHAPTER FIVE

THE SECRET NANAIMO BAR INGREDIENTS

When we got back to my room, I took out my magnifying glass and stared at the Nanaimo bar. The top chocolate layer looked just like any other Nanaimo bar I had ever seen. The yellow custard layer was equally familiar and the bottom layer looked as though it had the proper amounts of cocoa, coconut and almonds. I couldn't see anything that distinguished it from any other Nanaimo bars.

"It appears to be an everyday normal Nanaimo bar," I announced.

"Do you think there's an ingredient in the recipe that's turning people into Coronation-Street-watching-zombies?"

I raised my finger. "A good scientist never jumps to conclusions. Maybe Coronation Street is turning people into zombies. Or moon tides could be involved. We must keep our minds completely open to exponential possibilities."

"Okay, Einstein!" She sounded a little miffed.

If she was angry, the best thing to do was to get her talking. "Tell me everything you know about Nanaimo bars. Every single thing!"

"Well, since Joyce Hardcastle is my third aunt twice removed, I think I can answer that." Mrs. Hardcastle's recipe won the Ultimate Nanaimo Bar Recipe back in 1986, bringing her worldwide fame. Sophia used any excuse to bring up the fact that she was related to her.

"Some people think Nanaimo bars were sent over from England as gifts for miners during the coal-mining days of Nanaimo. Others say the bar first popped up in the 1930s in a recipe. But the Nanaimo bar's first documented appearance is in recipe books from the late 1950s. These recipe books were – "

"Uh, may I interrupt your speech?"

"You asked!"

"I know. I know. I just want you to see this." I handed her the magnifying glass.

Her eyes widened when she saw what I had seen.

"It's moving. I mean, the top layer is moving. Slowly."

She pulled the glass away. "It looks like normal Nanaimo bar topping." She stared through the magnifying glass again. "But it's clearly moving as though there are millions of mobile pieces that make up that chocolate."

"Exactly!" I said. "Is it some kind of virus or miniature bug?"

I took out my tiny scalpel and scraped off a bit of the layer, carefully spread it on a slide and slid the glass plate into my microscope. I looked through the binocular eyepieces and adjusted several knobs until it all came in clear.

"What do you see?" Archimedes asked. "Archie wants to know."

I couldn't believe my eyes. The layer of chocolate was magnified 100x, looking as tasty as ever, but crawling through it were tiny, tiny black ants with tiny metallic legs.

"Nanotechnology," I said.

"What?" Sophia pushed me out of the way and stared through the microscope. "What am I looking at? Gross, they're moving. What are they?"

"As I said before, it's nanotechnology. Robots built on a molecular scale. They're only a cell or two wide. All programmed to perform a specific task."

"What task?" she asked.

"I don't know, but it would probably happen once you swallowed the bar. So I bet the task has something to do with whoever eats the Nanaimo bar. The Nano ants most likely get into the bloodstream and could go anywhere in the body. The lungs. The heart. The brain. What they do there is anyone's guess."

"That's gross and frightening. Nano ants inside people's bodies! Who would plant all these Nano-infected bars in households across Nanaimo?"

"Someone who has access to some very advanced technology. This is NASA stuff."

"Why would they do this to Nanaimo?"

"Why not?" I asked. "If you're going to do an experiment, Nanaimo is the perfect place. It's on an island. And most people don't know where it is. In fact, the Canadian government once forgot Nanaimo existed. But I digress."

Sophia put her hands on her hips and furrowed her brow. "I still don't get what the big plan is. Maybe Nanaimo is the stepping stone to taking over the whole world."

"Again, I remind you not to jump to conclusions. Let's go through what we know. One: There are Nanaimo bars that have been tampered with. Two: Those same bars were stolen by a hairy-armed woman. Three: The maker of the bars has access to some ultra-advanced technology."

"Don't forget the odd behaviours!"

"I was getting to that! Four: The Nanaimo bars seem to cause odd behaviours. Vacuuming and watching Coronation Street and..." I stopped. "Oh no."

"What?"

"Mom was vacuuming today and watching Coronation Street, just like Mrs. Schellinck. She might be infected."

"Not Mom. Not Mom!" Archimedes said.

I threw open the door, skidded around the corner, nearly slipping on the shag carpet (my parents have out-dated taste in carpet), bumped into the fridge, then dashed into the living room.

I suddenly saw the most unimaginably horrible thing.

CHAPTER SIX

ANOTHER MINDLESS VICTIM

Mom was dusting. She had somehow found one of those pink-and-purple feather dusters and was cleaning the top of the piano. She was also now wearing an apron. I had never seen her dust. Ever. Or wear an apron. It was against everything Mom stood for.

"Mom! Put down that duster!"

She stopped, looked at me and smiled so widely I thought the smile would stretch right off her face. "Gordon Whillickers, my favourite son!"

"I'm your only son. You know that! And why are you dusting?"

"Dusting is good. Cleanliness is good. Did you wash behind your ears? Did you brush your teeth?"

"Yes! Are you okay, Mom? Are you feeling sick?"

"I am perfectly fine, Gordon Whillickers."

The way she kept saying my name was freaking me out. She put her hands on her hips. "Hello, Sophia Morrison from a dwelling on Black Powder Trail. How are you? Did *you* wash behind your ears today?"

"Uh, I'm fine." Sophia stepped back a bit from Mom. "And yes, I did wash behind my ears."

"I am being a good mother. I must offer you treats. Would you two younglings like lemonade?" She nearly ran into the kitchen and we followed.

Sophia whispered, "I think something's wrong."

"Oh, something is definitely wrong! I'm worried!"

Mom pulled a pitcher of lemonade out of the fridge, then plunked it on the table. Next she got two glasses from the perfectly stacked dishes in the kitchen and filled them. "Here is the lemonade. And, of course, you must be hungry. How about…"

I knew what she was going to say.

"…some Nanaimo bars."

I put up my hands. "I'm full, Mom. So is Sophia. And we're not thirsty, either." I was starting to be freaked out to the extreme. She wasn't acting like my mom at all.

"Oh, growing children need food! They need sustenance. They need Nanaimo bars."

Just then the back door that leads to the garage swung open and Dad came in. His glasses were halfway down his nose and his hair was looking like a crow had tried to build a nest in it. He had grown a goatee because he thought it would make him look younger. He was home early from work at Whillickers and Stone, his architectural firm.

"I got your call, dear," he said. "What was the urgent matter you wanted to talk about?"

"Oh, that," Mom said. "It's a very important topic. Extremely important. Sorry to interrupt your productive work cycle for this but…" She swung the plate towards Dad. "Have a Nanaimo bar."

"What?" Dad said. He stared at the bars for a moment, then reached out towards the plate.

"No, Dad, don't!" I exclaimed. I sprang into action. Well, sprang is perhaps the wrong word, it was more like I tripped into action. I tried to jump for the plate, but my feet got caught up in the carpet and my legs got tangled up with each other, and I missed the plate and did a belly flop on the floor, landing so hard the china rattled in the cabinet.

I rolled over, my guts and every bone in my body aching. "Nnnooo!"

Too late. Dad was looking down at me, a half-eaten Nanaimo bar in his hand and a smudge of chocolate on his cheek. He always was a messy eater.

"What's gotten into Gordon?" he asked, chewing.

Then he suddenly grimaced and shook his head. He put his hand on his stomach. "What's gotten into me?"

"There's something wrong with the Nanaimo bars," I wheezed, slowly getting to my feet. "They're bad!"

"Gordon, my favourite son," Mom said. "Nanaimo bars can't ever be bad."

Dad looked from me to Mom then back to the Nanaimo bars. "I have to go to the washroom," he announced. He did appear to be turning pale. "When I get back out, I want answers. I'm working on a very important project and I shouldn't be here right now just for snack time."

Mom looked down at me. "You should ambulate more carefully from now on, son."

"Ambulate? What? What's going on with you, Mom?"

"What's. Going. On?" Her face became extremely quizzical. "Gordon Whillickers …" Then for a moment I thought I saw my old mom there. She narrowed her eyes.

"What is happening? Why do I have an apron on?" She touched her head. "And curlers in my hair?" Then she spotted the plate of Nanaimo bars in her hand. "And why do I feel like I have to eat a Nanaimo bar right this instant?" She snatched one up and with a horrified look threw the whole thing in her mouth. A moment later she smiled.

"Did you clean up your bedroom, son?" she asked.

"Mom." I was shaking. My knees knocked together. Sophia put her hand on my shoulder, perhaps to steady me.

Dad came out of the washroom. He had shaved off his goatee and put gel in his hair so that it was slicked back. He looked like Fonzie in that really old show, Happy Days.

"Gordon, my favourite son, why don't we go outside and play catch?"

CHAPTER SEVEN

THE WEIRDNESS DEEPENS

I ran to my room. Sophia followed and closed the door behind her.

"Gordy, what's wrong?" Archimedes asked. "Archie wants to know: what's wrong?"

"Everything!" I answered. "Mom and Dad are mindless robots."

"What do you think is happening?" Sophia asked.

"I don't know!" I was feeling a tightness in my chest so I reached for my ventilator. But it wasn't my asthma acting up. I was genuinely worried. What if they always stayed that way? Mom was addicted to Coronation Street and vacuuming. We'd have the cleanest, craziest house on Cilaire Drive.

"You said we have to analyze the data."

"They've been turned into robots! That's the data!"

Sophia grabbed my arm. "Get ahold of yourself!" she shouted. "Remember, you're Gordon Whillickers, the smartest kid in Nanaimo."

I looked at her hand, felt the tight grip. I took a deep breath. "You're right. You're absolutely and completely right."

"Well, I was kidding about the smartest part. Second smartest."

"What?" Then she smiled. "Thank you for snapping me out of my panic-stricken state," I said.

"Anytime."

My brain was back at work, all pistons firing. I examined the mysteries, trying to determine other things that could have happened. "What about your parents?" I asked. "Did they get any Nanaimo bars?"

Sophia covered her mouth, her face displaying shock. "Yes! They could be eating them right now. We have to get over there!"

A knock at the door silenced both of us.

"Gordon," Mom said, "are you doing your homework?"

"Did you wash behind your ears?" Dad asked. "Let's play ball."

"After I'm done my homework," I said and they shuffled away. I had to fix this somehow.

"Let's get going," I said.

Moments later, Sophia and I climbed out the window. I brought my backpack with me and Archimedes clung to my shoulder. "Walk quiet," he whispered. We ran down the street and then made our way towards Sophia's house.

The view of Departure Bay opened up before us. A ferry was coming in from the mainland, tooting its horn, hundreds of passengers watching as they neared the dock. They didn't know the danger they might be getting into: the first thing any tourist did when they got to Nanaimo was to try a Nanaimo bar.

I followed Sophia into her house, Archimedes flapping his wings. "Gordy runs too fast," he said.

Sophia banged open the door and shouted, "Dad!"

Her father was a writer and he was home all the time. As far as I could tell, he was never really working but spent most of his time with a cloudy, deep-thought look on his face.

"Dad!"

Mr. Morrison came around the corner. He was wearing a suit, and had on a tie. I'd always seen him in blue jeans and a t-shirt. His hair was slicked back, just like my dad's.

"Sophia Camryn Morrison," he said, "my favourite daughter."

"Not you too," she whispered.

"I see you've brought Gordon Whillickers from Cilaire Drive. Are you two decagenarians hungry? Would you like some Nanaimo bars?"

"Noooooo!" She put her hands to the sides of her head. "NOOOOO!"

"They're good for you," he said.

"Thank you, Mr. Morrison," I said. "May I take the whole plate?"

"Of course! I have more in the kitchen. Now excuse me, I have to go view Front Page Challenge."

We watched as he flicked on the TV and an old show that was popular before I was born came on. In it a group of people had to guess who the special guest was.

"Yes, you're right!" the special guest on the show yelled to the panelists. "I am Vincent Price. Ha ha ha!" I loved old horror movies, so I knew exactly who Vincent Price was – the king of horror movies.

"I can't believe it!" Sophia was pulling on her hair. "My father is a mindless zombie."

"I think there's hope. Remember my mother nearly snapped out of it for a few seconds? I think they have to keep eating the Nanaimo bars to stay robotified."

"Robotified? Did you just make that up?"

"No, it's in the dictionary. Anyway, I thought if we took the plate away, at least he couldn't eat these ones."

We went into the backyard, carefully carrying the plate. I set it down on a bench. No flies landed on it – they were smart enough to stay away.

"We're gonna get whoever is doing this," Sophia said. "We have to. They can't just go around turning people's parents into robots."

"I wonder how big the whole plan is," I said.

"Archie thinks the plan is massive," Archie said. "Scary massive."

I stroked his head. He looked worried too. At least they didn't seem to be trying to turn birds into robots. "Archimedes might be right. What if those bars were delivered to every house in Nanaimo and eaten by every boy, girl, woman and man?"

"Is it possible?"

"Well, it could just be our neighbourhood."

"We should check."

We both got up and walked out the side gate of the backyard and onto the street. I looked down the road. All the trees were green. It was another beautiful Nanaimo day, complete with birds chirping.

"Where do we look?" Sophia asked.

"Well, school's out, so we can't go there. Maybe if we head up to the mall. If people are acting weird, we'll know. I mean weirder than usual."

A Honda drove by and the man inside waved.

Nanaimoites are friendly, but they don't always wave to everyone. Maybe it was a robot thing to do. Another car went by and the woman driving waved. A third car putted past us, a teenage boy with long hair and a bandana. He waved, his speakers pumping out classical music.

"Did you hear the music he was playing?" I asked. "They must be zombies!"

"We can't know for sure. Maybe he's just rebelling."

We stood on the corner for another minute. Just then Jackson Reid motored up to us on his tricycle, his legs pumping at a blur.

"Jackson! Jackson!" I yelled as he shot past us, grunting out muffler sounds as though he were riding a Harley-Davidson motorcycle. He sounded like any other five-year-old I'd ever seen. "Jackson!"

He skidded to a stop and looked back at us. "Gordon Whillickers! Sophia Morrison! You are residents of this specific neighbourhood. It is a pleasure to see you. I must go home to watch Friendly Giant. You should do your homework."

Then he pumped the pedals again, zipping towards his house.

"All of Nanaimo has gone completely bananas," Sophia said.

"Yep, we may be the only sane people left."

CHAPTER EIGHT

THE RETURN OF THE BIG HAIRY

We retreated to Sophia's backyard. The sun was getting brighter and hotter, one of those days when you could fry eggs on your forehead – or your bald spot, if you had one. We didn't want to go back in the house for a drink, so Sophia turned on the garden hose and we each had a sip. Even Archimedes leaned off my shoulder and wet his tongue.

We lounged in the lawn chairs. The Nanaimo bars hadn't even melted the slightest in the heat.

"What are we gonna do?" Sophia asked.

I wiped sweat from my forehead. "Well, there are several things to do in a situation like this…uh…but I just can't think of any of them."

"We have to inform the police."

"It's entirely probable that they are also robotified zombies. They do seem to like Nanaimo bars."

"Well, we'll e-mail the city councillors."

"They also are likely zombies."

"Then…" She seemed stumped. "…then we'll tell the librarians."

I thought about this for a moment. "Hmmmm." I started to think aloud. "They are smart enough to figure out that something odd is going on. On the other hand, they also do tend to like Nanaimo bars. I don't want to say all of them do, but I have been to several library events where they served Nanaimo bars, so that would lead to the conclusion that – "

"Archie must interrupt," Archimedes interjected, his claws digging into my shoulder, "a hairy guest is here."

"Sssh, Archie. I'm trying to make a point. Anyway, librarians are cerebral, as I was saying, but the sweets are their Achilles heel, so to speak. Do you know who Achilles was?"

Sophia gave me a swat. "Of course I do. A Greek hero who was invulnerable except for his heel."

"Exactly. Well my point is, you may have – "

"Big hairy!" Archimedes interjected. "Big hairy!"

"What are you squawking about?" I said.

A cloud crept over the sun and I shivered. I realized slowly that it wasn't a cloud – it was a shadow. Something large was looming behind us.

"Uh, Sophia…"

"What?"

"Were you expecting visitors?"

I turned slowly to see that the plate of Nanaimo bars was gone. I kept turning. The gate at the back of the yard was open and swinging.

"The Nanaimo bar thief!" I shouted and jumped to my feet, making Archimedes flap his wings.

"Where?" Sophia asked, but instead of answering I was already on my way, sneakers pounding the lawn. As we shot past the flower garden, I saw that the tulips had been knocked aside by the thief, and there were more giant footprints. For a big hairy lady, she could really move fast.

I dashed through the back gate with Sophia a few steps behind me. We ran out onto the street. One of those big green garbage cans had been knocked over, so we stopped there and gawked around. There was no sign of our thief.

"Which way?" I said.

"Archie closed his eyes," he said. "Too scared."

Stumped again! Sophia and I ran a bit further ahead, then I slapped myself on the side of the head, rattling my own slow brain.

"Archimedes!" I shouted, feeling like the commander of an air squadron. "Launch and follow our target."

"10-4! 10-4!" he said, then he was up in the air. He circled above us three or four times, then took off to the south, in the direction of the docks.

We ran like Olympic pentathletes, down the street, through backyards, apologizing to people as we jumped over their flower beds. Old Lady Busbee (she really was old) shook her hoe at us. But we kept on.

Then I lost sight of Archimedes.

"Do you see him?" I shouted.

Sophia skidded to a stop. I was surprised her hiking boots hadn't started to smoke. "No, he's disappeared."

We dashed around, cranking our necks, nearly bumping into fence posts and lamp standards. Finally Archimedes came out of the sun like a fighter plane, swooped over us, and croaked out, "Hurry now! Hurry fast!"

We hurried fast. We dashed down through brush and overgrown property that seemed to be abandoned. We slid into the gulley that ran all the way down to the beach. Somewhere in the back of my mind I heard my mom say, "Don't play in the gulley!" How many times had she shouted that at me as a kid? But I had to carry on. The grass was high. We ducked under branches, slewed our way through mud and onto harder, rocky ground.

A low, rumbling BWWWWWOOOOOOOOOOOOGGAHH-HHHH shook the ground and nearly stopped my heart.

It was the foghorn from a ferry coming in from Vancouver. We were obviously close to the docks, though I couldn't see through the foliage. It sounded like it was right on top of us.

We cut through the jungle-like fauna. Archimedes let out a squawk here and there so that we could keep track of him. It was like having our very own sonar machine. The leaves were just too thick to see through.

Then we skidded to a stop, because Archimedes was sitting on a branch, pointing down with one wing. Below him was an open hole. Broken boards that looked as if they'd been around since the 1800s littered the edge.

"Down there!" Archimedes said, huffing. "Down there!"

We looked down into the hole. There was only enough light to see a few feet, but the hole seemed to curve and then head away from us. A rotted wooden ladder stuck out over the lip.

"Our thief seems to have a getaway tunnel," I said.

"Well, I'm not going down there."

"C'mon," I said. "What could happen?"

CHAPTER NINE

INTO THE DARKNESS

I reached around on my belt pack and found my mini-flashlight. I shone it down the hole. It was actually a tunnel.

"I repeat: I will not be going down there," Sophia said. She peered over the edge as though she expected a horde of vampire bats to come flocking out. Okay, I know vampire bats don't live this far north, but that is the exact look she had on her face.

I leaned a little closer and one small, ordinary bat did come shooting out.

"Extremely dark," Archimedes said. He whistled.

I was as scared as Sophia looked, but I didn't want to show it. "We have to get to the bottom of this."

"The tunnel?"

"You know what I mean! Why our parents are robitified zombies. We can't have them stay that way forever. Besides…" and I paused to be more dramatic, "you're not chicken are you?"

"Chicken?" She practically pushed me aside and climbed down to the tunnel floor. "Get that light on. Let's go."

I followed, surprised that the old ladder was actually holding me. The last rung snapped like a toothpick and I slipped, twisting my ankle a bit.

"Are you okay?" Sophia asked.

I put weight on my leg. "It feels fine. I was just surprised, that's all."

"You shouldn't eat so many Nanaimo bars."

I chuckled. My chuckles echoed around us.

Archimedes flapped down to my shoulder. I pointed the flashlight around, illuminating several chunks of wood.

"Archie not like the smell," Archimedes said.

It did smell as though people were tossing their garbage into the hole, but I couldn't see any debris. In the darkness my skin grew clammy. I was a little freaked out. What if the thief was violent? But she had been running, so she must be afraid of *us*.

The flashlight showed me that the hole curved away and down at a sharp angle so that we could slide right to the end if we weren't careful. There were large support blocks, all expertly cut, holding the tunnel together.

"It's running straight towards the water," I said.

"I think it's a mining tunnel." At once I knew she was onto something. The wood supports looked ancient and Nanaimo was once a coal-mining town – our city was really built on an anthill of coal mines.

"You're right, Sophia. You're smarter than you look." She gave me a playful shove that would leave a bruise. I rubbed my shoulder and squinted around. "But it doesn't go into the hill. That's where the coal would have been. It goes straight ahead towards the bay. Let's keep going."

We slid and stepped and slid our way down the path. Twice I had to grab the wall for support, surprised by how cold and wet it was. Mould and moss grew like a green carpet beneath my feet.

"We're spelunking now," Sophia whispered.

"I'm sorry to correct you," I whispered, patiently, "but actually we're *caving*. Spelunkers are amateurs and we are professionals. They're called cavers. Though we could also be speleologists – people who study caves."

"Thanks, Gordo, but I guess I'm the caver, since I have hiking boots on and you only have running shoes."

She was right. If I'd been fully prepared, I'd be clad in my warm caving clothes, knee pads, gloves and my helmet (with a miner's light). Instead I was in a cotton τ-shirt, holding a skinny flashlight. Cotton sucked up the moisture, making me colder. If only I'd known I'd be caving today, I would've brought all my equipment. At least I had a small medical kit on my belt. And my protractor, in case I needed to measure something.

"Anyway, technically we're in a tunnel, so I guess we're actually just walking," Sophia said. I'd had enough arguing.

"Let's get going," I whispered. I was whispering because I didn't want the roof to fall in. Even the slightest loud sound can be dangerous in an old tunnel.

We went down, down, down, all the time still able to walk upright. Only once in awhile did I have to duck to miss a beam. Whoever had built this tunnel had done an expert job.

Soon the ceiling of the tunnel began to drip. Some of it had turned into stalactites. The dripping became a little annoying – it was like having ice hit your skin. I shivered.

My flashlight blinked out.

"Turn it on," Sophia whispered.

"I'm trying." I hit it and jiggled the on/off switch. Finally it came back on, but my heart was beating faster now. I didn't want to try and find my way out without any light. At least there didn't appear to be any side tunnels.

We pushed on, now splashing through an inch of water. "We must be halfway across the bay," Sophia whispered.

We struggled on. Archimedes was silent the whole time, but his beak was clacking as he shivered.

Finally the tunnel began to go upwards and this gave me more strength. I saw light ahead and breathed a giant sigh of extra-happy relief. I hadn't realized how claustrophobic I was getting.

At the end of the tunnel was another ladder. We climbed it and dragged ourselves out into the open. We were surrounded by trees, in a spot so well hidden that when I looked back I couldn't see the tunnel entrance. I nearly fell in, searching for it.

"We're on Newcastle Island," Sophia said.

"Yeah, it's good to be out of the cold." I could see Nanaimo across the bay from us. "I think we're near Midden Bay. The old mine shafts are in this area."

Because I'd grown up looking across to Newcastle Island, I knew a lot about it. For instance, I knew that the Salish First Nations had once had villages here and that coal was discovered in 1849 and that there are mine shafts remaining from those days. The island even had a fish-salting operation and a sandstone quarry and later became a pleasure resort. In the end it was turned into a provincial park. Dad and I camp here every summer as a Father/Son trip.

Thinking of Dad made me feel a little sad. What if he was stuck being a robotified zombie forever? We'd never camp here again. He and Mom wouldn't take me to Victoria for the Vancouver Island IQ science convention every year. They'd just spend their time telling me to wash behind my ears.

"We better get a move on," I said. We walked straight ahead until we found one of the hiking trails. "I have no idea where this thief is. Maybe she lives secretly on Newcastle Island, one of those hippie types who never shaves. That would explain the hairy arms. But where would she hide?"

"I know," Sophia said.

"You do?" I nearly spat out the words. I didn't mean to sound so surprised. "But how?"

She pointed down. A Nanaimo bar was lying on the ground. "Well, notice how the Nanaimo bar skidded to the west? I'd say our culprit is this way." She pointed.

She was right. A few meters away I spotted a footprint in the soft mud. "She has to be a hippie," I announced, "she's definitely not wearing any shoes."

We went another hundred meters without spotting another clue. Then I sent Archimedes into the air with a "Search and find!" command.

"Archie will search! Archie will find!" He took off

flying amongst the Douglas fir. Twice he nearly brained himself, but he flapped on.

"Follow Archie!"

We followed. I lost track of direction but soon I heard the swell of the waves against the shore and the land rose higher. Archimedes began to circle around the sandstone cliffs and we caught up to him. He was hovering in place and when we got there I saw a cave.

"I'll go in," I said. "You stay here in case there's trouble. Then...uh...run for help."

"What? No, you stay here."

She had that stubborn look in her eyes. "Fine," I said. "We'll both enter the cave. If anything goes haywire, it's your fault. These hippies can be crazy!"

We climbed up the sandstone. A cloud had covered the sun and now there was a slight sprinkling of rain, just like that – a typical Nanaimo day. My feet slipped on the rocks and I banged my knee, but didn't let out a whimper. I didn't want our thief to know we were coming.

Struggling up to the mouth of the cave, we looked inside. It was totally dark. Archimedes swooped down and landed on my shoulder. We took a few steps in, but even by squinting I couldn't see much further.

"Use your flashlight, Einstein," Sophia whispered.

I dug it out of my belt, fumbled with the switch, but

it wouldn't come on. "Stupid thing," I whispered. Maybe I hadn't recharged the batteries. Sophia started to make a grumbling noise beside me.

"Stop making that noise," I whispered.

"What noise?"

"The stomach-growling noise."

"I'm not making that noise. You are."

I suddenly felt a chill. I hit the flashlight desperately and it came on.

A leering, ugly, monstrous face loomed right in front of us.

CHAPTER TEN

BIG, HAIRY...HUNGRY?

"**B**ig hairy monster!" Archimedes shouted.

He was right. Standing before us, about seven feet tall and all covered with hair, was some sort of ape-like creature. Its eyes were narrowed and it looked angry enough to tear us each in two.

"Back away slowly," I whispered. "Don't show any fear."

We both took a slow simultaneous step backwards. The monster's eyes glared from me to Sophia and back to me. We took another slow simultaneous step.

The monster blinked. Its two arms shot out and grabbed us by the shoulders.

"YURRRRNOTGO!" it growled.

I didn't know what to do. Archimedes had jumped off my shoulder and was flapping around at the mouth of the cave. "Get help!" I said, but he squawked and circled around. I tried to pull away. The creature's hand squeezed like a giant vice grip.

"Sophia," I whispered. "I'm sorry I was sometimes snotty to you."

"Be quiet!" she whispered. "Use your brilliant brain to think of a way out of this."

I couldn't see any obvious means of escape. I looked at the monster's teeth. They were flat and square. "Maybe it's a vegetarian. We might not get eaten."

"Oh great. It could still snap us in two like twigs."

"EYEWONTEACHOO," the creature growled. It almost sounded like words.

"Pardon?" I said.

"I. WON'T." It paused. "EAT. YOU."

"Oh!" The words suddenly made sense. "You won't eat us! Oh, that's great news. Did you hear that, Sophia, the monster won't eat us. And it speaks English."

"That's very kind of you not to eat us," Sophia said. "We don't taste very good anyway."

"Don't move!" the monster said. It let me go and I absolutely wanted to made a break for it, but I couldn't abandon Sophia. The creature reached across us into the darkness and I heard a *click*.

A light came on. It had flicked on a switch. I glimpsed the painted fingernails I'd seen before. The creature was hairy from head to toe, the thick fur a reddish brown and smelling like pine scent. It was wearing a T-shirt that had the letters BHM on it and also a grass skirt that could have been imported from Hawaii. Behind it was a mountain of Nanaimo bars.

I glanced at her large feet. Any field goal kicker would be pleased to have feet that gigantic. And then my brilliant brain figured out exactly what – who – we were face to face with: a sasquatch. A Bigfoot! How many cryptozoologists (the people who study legendary animals) would want to be in my shoes right now? I'd gladly trade.

"Lemonade?" the sasquatch asked.

"Uh," I said. "Sure."

She let go of Sophia, took a clay container out of a cubbyhole in the cave wall and poured two clay cups of lemonade. She handed one to me and the other to Sophia. I noticed that the hair on her head, which was reddish and quite long, had been carefully braided.

I sipped the lemonade. It was rich with sugar and a real lemon flavour. The best lemonade I had ever tasted.

"So, uh…how…speak you English?" I asked.

The sasquatch raised her eyebrows. "How did I learn to speak English? Is that what you're asking? I first learned it from the miners on this island. Over a hundred years ago."

"A hundred years?" I nearly sputtered out some of my lemonade.

"Yes. My kind live many hundreds of your years." She drank from her own mug. The whole situation somehow all seemed so civilized. "By the way, I should introduce myself. I am Cheryl."

"Cheryl? That's your name?" I suddenly realized how rude I sounded. "I mean, it's a nice name."

The sasquatch – Cheryl – laughed, a deep gurgling sound. "Well, in sasquatch it's Cherak-kee-ka-to-kuy-kiv-keequa-qua-qua-quo-que-qua-yl but that's probably too long for you to remember. So Cheryl it is."

"Oh. I'm Gordon and this is Sophia."

"I'm Archie the magnificent!" Archimedes shouted as he settled on my shoulder again. Like I said, he isn't modest.

Cheryl whistled several short bursts and Archimedes replied, then they both chuckled.

"You're really a sasquatch?" Sophia asked.

"That's one of the names you humans use. We call ourselves *Sasa-quatcha-sasaquitcha-saso-songnocktorioruses*. But again that's a little too long for you simple humans to remember, so the Chehalis people shortened it to *sokqueatl*, which a teacher turned into sasquatch."

"Where did you get your nail polish?" Sophia asked.

Cheryl displayed her fingers. "It's an ancient sasquatch secret. Lots of pigments and special ash. Only I know where to get them and the proper mixture."

Nail polish? Next they'd be talking about hairstyles. I had to ask some important questions. "How did you get electricity in your cave?"

"I have a turbine that's powered by waves. Very simple technology. We've been using it for about eight hundred years now."

"Eight hundred years! But I thought you sasquatches were all...uh..."

"Monsters? Savage cave creatures? Dumb?" She let out another friendly laugh. "I'm used to that. You humans always judge sasquatches by their covers. Nah. We're way ahead of you on so many things. We just use what we need from the earth."

"What does the BMH stand for on your T-shirt?" Sophia asked.

Cheryl looked down at her shirt. "That? Oh, my son got me this shirt. BHM. It means Big Hairy Monster. But to him it's Big Hairy Mom. He thought he was being funny. If I'd known I was getting guests, I would have dressed up. We don't get too many guests out here."

"But," I asked, searching through my head for folklore about sasquatches, "I thought you sasquatches only lived on the mainland."

"Vancouver Island and area is where we come to retire. The mainland is soooo busy. All those hunters. And the young sasquatches, well who can keep up with them? All their new hairstyles and cedar flute rap songs. My son has a band that is quite popular among our kind. Can't stand to listen to the stuff myself. Anyway, you have been very persistent in tracking me down. Admirable, actually." She paused and motioned towards the back of the room.

"I suppose you want to know the answer to that burning question: What the heck is going on with all these Nanaimo bars?"

CHAPTER ELEVEN

TURN LEFT AT THE BLUE SUPERGIANT

"First," Cheryl said, "and brace yourselves, we are not alone."

"What?" I looked around the cave. "What do you mean? Is there someone invisible here? I read sasquatches can turn invisible. Is that what you mean?"

Cheryl laughed. "Invisible? No, we can't. We just blend in with the background. It's called camouflage. Plus we don't zip around on ATVs, so we're harder to hear and spot. What I mean about not being alone is that there are visitors from another planet here."

"Which planet?" Sophia asked. She was the UFO and alien species expert of Nanaimo. Well, no one else had claimed the title. "The Arcturus system? The Alpha Centauri cluster?"

"No. The good ol' Deneb system. It's about 1800 light years away and forms the upper part of the Southern Cross. It's a bright star. Actually a blue supergiant, to be precise. I don't know much about the Denebians, but this is their technology." She scooped up a handful of metal ants from the table. They were all apparently dead or out of energy. "These are segmentoids. A lot like superpowered ants. They run on lemonade. If I poured a glass on them, they'd all come to life and try to complete their tasks."

"That's some pretty advanced tech," I said. I was still trying to wrap my mind around the fact that there were aliens in Nanaimo. I mean, why us of all places? Why not Moose Jaw? Or Wolfville? I wasn't completely surprised, though. I've spent many hours looking at the stars with my telescope expecting someone to wave back.

"Well, they're taking Nanaimo's name far too seriously," Sophia said.

"What do you mean?" I asked.

"The aliens. They must know that Nanaimo's name comes from the Coast Salish word, *Sney-ny-mo*. It means 'the meeting place.' Obviously the aliens have done their research. They've come to meet us here."

"Sometimes, Sophia, you know way too much," I said, rolling my eyes. I turned to Cheryl. Now that I was over the shock of meeting a sasquatch, I noticed that she really did have a very pleasant face, with wide, caring eyes. When she smiled, her face lit up. "What do you think they want with us?" I asked.

"That's what I've been trying to figure out," Cheryl said. "I'm always protecting Nanaimo. I spend a lot of time snooping around to be sure things are okay. I've kind of adopted your city."

"Our own guard sasquatch," Sophia said.

"I suppose you could say that." She shrugged. "I did stop the killer bee invasion last year."

"What killer bee invasion?" I asked.

"Exactly!" Cheryl smiled. "They never made it here. I keep my eyes open and my nose ready to smell. That's how I saw the Nanaimo bars being delivered throughout the city and started sniffing around. I had a feeling they were more than just normal Nanaimo bars."

I told her about my parents, Sophia's parents and everyone else we saw.

"That's very odd," Cheryl said. "I still don't know what the Denebians want here. In fact, out of all the alien races that have visited earth, they're the ones I know the least about."

"How many aliens have visited us?" Sophia asked.

"Eighty-seven different species," Cheryl said. "That's another thing we sasquatches do, is keep track of the alien visitors. We make sure they don't take anything too large back home with them. Like our atmosphere, for instance."

"I guess we humans owe you sasquatches a lot," I said.

Cheryl shrugged her hairy shoulders. "Just our job. Anyway, I'm not even sure what these aliens look like. I haven't seen one face to face. And I don't know what they want. Maybe they're using Nanaimo as an experiment and they plan to take over the world from there. Or at least Canada."

"How do we find out?" I asked.

"We'll have to go back to Nanaimo and scout around. It'll be dangerous work."

"I'm not worried," Sophia said. Her jaw was set. I knew she was thinking of her parents.

I set my jaw too. "Me either."

"The alien or aliens know I'm here," Cheryl said. "They've figured out someone is stealing the Nanaimo bars. Twice little robots have come to try and put me out of action."

"Out of action?" I repeated.

She nodded.

I swallowed. "Whatever. We have to save our parents. And everyone else in Nanaimo."

CHAPTER TWELVE

GUY LAFLEUR AND ALIEN TECHNOLOGY

We went back to the tunnel. Cheryl zipped through ahead of us and we struggled to keep up. For someone so large, she moved with the speed and grace of an antelope. Soon we had climbed up into the outskirts of Nanaimo.

Everything was eerily silent. I looked back through the bushes and down at the docks where a ferry was waiting, but not a single car or person was moving. Usually the docks were a hubbub of action, but something had obviously gotten to them.

"They've all been robotified," I said. "All the tourists, the businessmen, the businesswomen, the whale watchers.

They must be getting Nanaimo bars the moment they step off the ship."

"It's like we've been cut off from the rest of the world," Sophia said.

"Archie thinks this situation is weird," Archimedes commented. "Very weird."

"This is getting out of hand," Cheryl said. "I wish there was time to summon reinforcements. Bert would be a big help now."

"Bert?" I asked.

"Oh, he's a yeti. They know a lot more about alien invasions and such. But he's in the Himalayas and needs at least two weeks warning. We're gonna have to do this ourselves."

"Uh, do you have a plan?" I asked. "I'm pretty good at plans, but I don't have one right now. We could work on one together."

"Why don't we keep walking?" Cheryl said. "I think better when I'm moving."

"I want to check on my parents," I said. "Maybe there's a clue there."

We walked up the hill to Cilaire Drive. The streets were empty. No one was driving or walking around. Birds chirped and occasionally there was a dog bark. I glanced at my watch. Maybe Coronation Street was on.

Mr. Reid, our neighbour, was out in his front yard.

He was a science teacher and had helped me with a few of my experiments. He was also an avid gardener, who grew every species of plant imaginable in his yard. He'd spent hours nurturing them to life and would spend hours telling you about them.

Right now he was running his electric lawn mower over his garden. Flowers of all different colours were spitting out the side of the mower. It was a flower massacre – petals, stems and stamens were chopped into pieces and scattered across the yard.

I couldn't help myself. I ran over to him. "Mr. Reid! Mr. Reid! What are you doing? You're killing your flowers."

He didn't stop mowing. "Green grass, perfectly cut. Straight lines. Must plant green grass here and make lawn perfect and green. Each blade exactly the same height."

Then he looked up at Cheryl. I thought seeing a sasquatch would shock him out of whatever odd state of mind he was in, but he just pointed at her and said, "Young lady, you need curlers in your hair!"

At that moment, his wife came around the corner, wielding a Whippersnipper, chopping the heads off any remaining flowers. She suddenly dropped the device and turned to Mr. Reid. "Dear!"

I hoped she had snapped out of her trance.

"Dear!" she repeated. "The hockey game is on. You better watch it!"

Mr. Reid joined her and they practically scampered back into their house. I turned away. It was obvious they were robotified too.

We went into my house. Mom was vacuuming again and she had curlers in her hair, just like the woman on Coronation Street. My knees nearly buckled. She waved to us, a silly smile on her face, but didn't stop or even notice Cheryl.

Dad was wearing a suit, sitting up straight in his chair, watching a hockey game. His tie was perfectly tied and his hair perfectly gelled and parted in a perfect straight line. I had never seen him watch hockey before, other than to comment that they got paid too much to fight like little boys. He never knew the score, couldn't tell you the names of the first line of the Vancouver Canucks or the Nanaimo Clippers. And here he was watching every moment as though it was the most important event in the history of television. He didn't look away from the screen.

The game looked old. They must have been replaying it.

"That's the Chicago Blackhawks versus Montreal!" Sophia said. "I've seen that game before. It's from the 1970s. There's Guy Lafleur!"

The hockey game was interrupted by a commercial. It was for the Bastion, a fortified tower that the Hudson's Bay Company had built in Nanaimo way back in 1853. The ad talked about artifacts and exhibits and the cannon that fired at noon every day. They also asked for donations, saying, "Send your money and your specialized thoughts to the Bastion." I'd never seen the Bastion ask for money before. And how would we send thoughts? How very odd.

Even odder, this commercial was followed by another that just had a frog on the screen. It was a red-legged frog, a *rana aurora*, in case you're wondering about its Latin name. They are common to ponds and slow streams here on the island. I once did a paper on frogs, that's why I know so much. About frogs. Well, about everything, actually. Anyway, the frog just stared at the screen, not even blinking. It was the strangest ad I'd ever seen. Maybe it was for a cellphone or something. Then a voice said, "DO NOT HARM FROGS. THAT IS A COMMAND."

I looked at Dad. He continued staring unblinkingly at the screen. I would swear he was hypnotized.

Then hockey was right back on. I had hoped he and Mom would break out of this trance. They were my heroes – well, when they weren't telling me what to do.

We scooted out into the backyard and I caught a deep breath. Sophia put her hand on my shoulder.

"We'll save them, somehow," she said. "My parents too. Everyone."

"This is very odd," Cheryl said. "The shows on TV appear to be some sort of mind-programming device. I would guess that they're using the TV to send subliminal messages to your parents' brains."

"Subliminal means below the threshold of consciousness," I explained to Sophia.

"I know what subliminal means!" She poked me in the ribs.

"There are over 70,000 people in Nanaimo," I said. "Assuming even 70% of them are in this odd state of mind, that's a lot of people."

"It's an army," Sophia said.

"Maybe," Cheryl said. "Or enough workers to build an artifact. I think we should take a look around. I assume your parents have a car."

"I'm not old enough to drive," I said.

"I'll do the driving," Cheryl laughed. "I'm plenty old enough."

CHAPTER THIRTEEN

THE BUZZ ABOUT BOWEN PARK

It turns out that sasquatches aren't the greatest drivers in the world. "This is nothing like steering a wagon," Cheryl said, grinding the gears in my dad's Volvo. I gritted my teeth as we jerked into third and out onto the Island Highway. The car roared until she found fourth gear.

Usually the highway was jam-packed with vehicles – families heading to Long Beach, logging trucks, campers, motorcyclers and cyclists – but we were the only ones on the pavement.

"There's nobody around," Sophia said. "It's downright spooky. They can't all be robotified, can they?"

Neither of us said anything.

We went downtown and zipped left and right, passing near the best fish-and-chip place in town. I started to salivate, realizing it had been ages since I'd had anything to eat. The ships were out in the harbour, not moving, and no one was walking around the promenade.

We shot past the Bastion, the old Hudson's Bay Company tower. I thought I saw smoke coming out of the top, but it was just the way the clouds looked. There were several antennas on the roof of the tower and a satellite dish pointing straight up. Maybe the scientists at Malaspina College were using it as a weather research station. A sign said "Closed for Repairs."

Nanaimo was a ghost town. The only action was when a bee hit our windshield and bounced off without leaving its insides smeared all over the glass. That was one tough bee!

We drove silently. Even Archimedes kept his beak shut, and we stopped in Bowen Park near the interpretive centre. Cheryl got out and we followed her across the parking lot.

"Well, they certainly have done their work. I tried to stop the distribution of Nanaimo bars, but I didn't realize how big this was. I should have called in the other sasquatches." She sounded quite upset.

"You did your best." Sophia patted Cheryl's massive shoulder.

"We have to find a way to stop it, now," Cheryl said. "We know the Nanaimo bars turn people into robots.

That they then wear curlers and vacuum if they're women, and they wear suits and watch sports if they're men. It's a puzzle. Why watch the same show at the same time? What is that going to accomplish? Ah, I, wait…I think I've figured it out."

"What?" I asked.

"What?" Sophia also asked.

"What? What?" Archimedes squawked.

"Well, it makes sense. The hairstyles from the seventies. The shows. The odd use of antiquated language." She paused. "Do you hear that?"

"Hear what?" I asked. The city was rather quiet. You could hear a pin drop.

"Oh, I forgot sasquatches have better hearing than you humans. I can hear your heartbeats. Anyway, there's a buzzing noise in the distance."

Archimedes began fidgeting on my shoulder. "Bad buzz! Bad buzz!" he squawked.

The buzzing grew louder. "I can hear it," I said. "It's – "

"Get down!" Cheryl threw herself at both of us, so we thumped to the ground just as I caught sight of about a hundred bumblebees coming straight at us. She covered us and I heard the impact of the bees as they thudded into her back like bullets.

"AAAH!" Cheryl cried out. "AAARGH!"

"Cheryl!" Sophia shouted. We couldn't move.

Cheryl shuddered. "Be...strong," she whispered, then she slumped and her weight held us against the ground. I felt as though I'd be smothered.

"She's been stung to death," Sophia said. "They must be killer bees."

They were still buzzing all around us, sounding like miniature helicopters.

"No, she's breathing," I said. "I can smell her dinner. Carrots."

"But we're going to be smothered. She's so heavy. I mean big!"

I tried to pull myself out, but she was like a slab of rock pressing us down.

The buzzing grew louder. It sounded like there were even more bees. Suddenly I could breathe more easily and could see light. Cheryl was being lifted up. But how? Was there a crane nearby?

She hovered a few inches above us, and Sophia and I just stared, not even thinking of rolling away. She could drop down and crush us. Suddenly, with a giant buzzing sound, she flew up another meter or so, then was carried across the park just above the height of the bushes.

There were about a thousand bumblebees hauling her through the air. We both sat up and stared in shock as she disappeared towards the south end of the park.

Sophia put her hands on her hips. "I wouldn't believe it if I hadn't seen it with my own eyes."

I was still standing there in shock when Archimedes swept down and landed on my shoulder. "Blumble! Blee!" he mumbled.

I looked over at him. He was holding a bumblebee in his mouth. Its wings had stopped moving. He dropped it into my hand. Its eyes were round and mechanical. It was in the shape of a bee, but obviously made of some sort of light metal. The wings were plastic.

"Alien bee robots," I said. "They know we're on to them and they hunted us down. If Cheryl hadn't stepped in front of their stingers, I bet all three of us would be out of commission right now."

"What do we do now?" Sophia asked.

"Archie suggests you run now!" Archimedes said.

"What?" And then I saw another swarm of bees was buzzing through Bowen Park, coming over the duck pond and straight at us.

CHAPTER FOURTEEN

DRIVER'S TEST

We took Archie's advice and ran, galloping through the grass. The buzzing grew louder and louder, like a jumbo jet was aiming straight at us. I stole a glance over my shoulder. The bees were in "V" formation, cutting down the wind resistance, and they were gaining fast. I nearly tripped over a clump of grass.

"To the car!" Sophia shouted. "We'll be safe there!"

I wasn't so sure. The bees looked like they could cut right through the car, but I turned towards the parking lot, jumped over a meridian and grabbed the door.

Which was locked.

"You locked the doors?" Sophia yelled.

"Well, someone could have stolen it!"

"It's a city full of robotified zombies."

I dug frantically through my pockets and came up with some lint, two loonies, and a rechargeable battery. But no key.

"They're almost here!"

At last I found the keys, pressed the "unlock" button, then I swung open the driver's door and threw myself in the front seat with Archimedes one flap behind me. Sophia hit the back seat and with a CLUNK CLUNK we pulled the doors shut.

A microsecond later the bees smacked into the car like hail. They began crawling around the windows, searching for a way in.

"Drive!" Sophia yelled. She had jumped into the front passenger seat and was putting on her seat belt.

"But I've never driven the car!"

"Just drive!"

"Drive like the wind!" Archimedes shouted.

I glanced over at the bees. Little saws were protruding out of their thoraxes. They were going to cut the glass.

I started the car, threw on my seat belt and hit the gas so hard my foot slipped. When I slammed it down again, I accidentally jammed on the brakes, making the car lurch.

"I meant drive away. Not drive crazy!"

I ignored her and stomped the gas again and we

roared onto Bowen Road. It didn't take that much skill to drive – I pressed the gas and the car went forward, hit the brakes and it stopped. I kept as close to the middle of the road as possible, glad there was no other traffic.

A few of the bees flicked off the car, but most were clinging to the windows, still sawing away.

"They're going to get in here soon," Sophia said.

I turned sharply and went to the back of a gas station and sped into an automatic car wash, without even putting in a token. The machine must have had a motion sensor, because it turned on and a second later water and brushes were wiping the bees from the car. They tried to dig in but the brushes were too strong.

And the car looked a lot cleaner.

I sped back onto the road, happy to be free.

I kept driving erratically, partly on purpose, hoping to throw any other bees off course.

"Where are we going?" Sophia asked.

"I have an idea."

"Oh no."

"Oh no? My ideas aren't that bad."

"Well, what is it?"

"It's this!" I said, trying to sound like an action movie star. I cranked the wheel and we squealed onto Commercial Street, then I cranked it again, jumped the curb, brushed by a thin tree and headed straight for the front doors of the Nanaimo Harbourfront Library.

"You're going to kill us!" Sophia said as I just missed a black old-style lamp and a big blue post that I assumed was designed to keep cars from crashing into the library.

"Archie is too young!" he shouted. "To die!"

I would have laughed at their fear but I couldn't remember which pedal was the brake and which was the gas and accidentally jammed my foot down on the accelerator. The car lurched ahead and I stomped both feet on the brake pedal, skidding and swerving around the bunker-like planter and stopping just short of smashing through the doors.

"There," I said, trying to keep the quavering from my voice. "We'll probably never get a chance to drive like that again."

"You call that driving?"

"Invigorating, wasn't it? Now let's get in the library. There's a few things I want to look up." I glanced all around. No sign of killer bees, or killer ants for that matter. Or even humans. The glass of the library doors reflected us back to us.

"Do you think the librarians have all been robotified?" Sophia asked.

"It's very likely." I cracked open the car door, stepped out and pushed open the library doors. Archimedes and Sophia were half a step behind.

The first thing I smelled was books. It was a newer library, but that good ol' book smell had taken over the building. It's the smell of knowledge, of stories, of oodles of information waiting to jump from the pages into a reader's brain. I took a deep breath. I could feel myself getting smarter already.

"Okay, why are we here?" Sophia asked.

"Well," I said. "Mom was watching Coronation Street, so was Mrs. Schellinck, and Dad watched a hockey game from the past. And your dad was watching Front Page Challenge. What's similar between them all?"

"They're all from the same time period," Sophia said. I was surprised. She really was smart. Not as smart as me, but close.

"Right, and that means – "

"This book will help us!" She had pulled out an oversized book called *The Massive History of Television*. She flipped quickly through it and found a whole section on Canadian television. "Here it is. Front Page Challenge ran from 1957-1995."

"Boy, people watched boring TV back then. Anyway, see if you can find what year Vincent Price, that scary guy with the scary voice, was on the show."

She scanned the episodes. "It was 1973."

"And what year did the Montreal Canadiens play the

Chicago Blackhawks for the Stanley Cup? Quick, look that up."

"1971 and 1973, those were the two times in the 70s."

"You didn't even look that up!"

"I like hockey."

"So they must be playing the 1973 shows. Why? What happened in 1973?"

"You don't know?" A gravelly, crackling, loud voice made Sophia drop the book and my heart nearly stopped. "What are they teaching you kids these days?"

CHAPTER FIFTEEN

THE YEAR WAS 1973

A t first I thought she was a witch from a Shakespearean play. She was pointing a twisted wooden wand at us and her grey hair poked out of her head in all directions. Her clothes were shabby and her eyes flashed with craziness and anger.

Then gradually I recognized that the stick was a walking stick and if the hair had been combed and her eyes normal she was Deborah Delgatty, the youth librarian. Or Deb the Bookhead as she liked to be called.

"Deborah Delgatty," I said. "Please put down your walking stick. It's us!"

"Really it is!" Sophia said.

"How can I know for sure?" Deborah asked. "Everyone in Nanaimo has been turned into nanobotanical automatons."

"Archie is real!" Archie shouted. "We are all real!"

"What's a nanobotanical automaton?" I asked.

"First, you answer me. What's your favourite TV show?" She shook the stick towards me. I thought she was going to knock me out. Had she gone batty? She'd always been so nice. Well, as long as we didn't have an overdue book.

"It's CSI," I said.

The stick swung towards Sophia and pointed at her.

"Buffy the Vampire Slayer," Sophia said.

"It's not The Friendly Giant, then?" she asked.

"I don't even know that show," I said.

She lowered the stick. "Good. You seem to have all your faculties." I couldn't say the same about her. "A nanobotanical automaton, to answer your question, is a human being who has been reduced to just automatic responses by an organic hybrid nanobot, most likely from an alien culture."

"Oh, you know about the Denebians too," I said.

"How do you have that information?"

"A sasquatch told us," Sophia said. We both expected Deborah to look at us like we were crazy.

"Oh, so you've met Cheryl. Good."

"You know her?" I said.

"Of course. We librarians have communicated with the sasquatches ever since the first library was built here in Nanaimo. They get to keep library books for three weeks. Anyway, where is Cheryl?"

We told her the whole story as quickly as possible. Several times her eyes widened and she looked extremely worried. She did say, "Oh dear" twice. Finally Sophia finished with, "And Gordon nearly drove right through the library."

"Oh dear," Deborah said. "Well, if Cheryl trusted you, then I'll have to trust you too. I need a few extra hands and legs. Come with me."

We followed her to a spot near the back of the library. "How come you're not a nanobotanical robot-ofied zombie?" I asked.

"I don't eat Nanaimo bars. I used to, but I was getting too much chocolate on book pages, so I swore off chocolate."

I nodded. She banged the floor three times with her walking stick. I was about to ask what was going on when I heard a gear start to grind and a humming noise, and suddenly the floor opened up, revealing a set of glowing stairs.

"Welcome to the real library. The true source of information. Please don't touch anything without permission."

Both of us kids had our eyes wide open. I'd walked over this spot a million times and had no idea there was a room below. We followed Deb down the stairs and around the corner. There was a large room, lit by bluish-green light. In one corner, in silver book racks, were books that looked older than Canada, and next to them was a high-tech touchpad screen, glowing bluish words that said *Direct Link to CSIS Database*. In another corner were several flickering monitors and in the farthest end was what appeared to be an experimental lab. There were several dissected Nanaimo bars, and glass jars of robot ants, bees, beetles and other odd items.

"This is amazing!" I said. "Amazing!"

"Does this phone really go directly to the Prime Minister?" Sophia was reaching towards a red phone.

"Yes, but it's disconnected right now. All land, air and sea communications are cut off by alien interference technology. Nanaimo is an island, so to speak."

"That's scary," I said.

"Oh, that's just the beginning." She flicked a switch and the monitors came on. One was showing that same hockey game, another flickered with Front Page Challenge, and the third a show I could only assume was The Friendly Giant.

"I've been trying to crack the code on these shows for the last twenty-four hours." She did look a little tired.

"Just seeing the programs on their own isn't bad for you, but from what I've put together, if you've consumed a Nanaimo bar, the nanobots go directly to your brain and climb into your occipital lobe. While you're watching one of these shows, you slip into a dream state and shoot out alpha waves."

"Alpha waves?" Sophia asked.

"They're brainwaves," I explained to her.

"Electromagnetic oscillations, to be more specific," Deb added. "Now imagine this. Every single citizen of Nanaimo sitting in front of their television set watching the same show, beaming their alpha waves to one central place."

"Is that what's happening?" I asked.

"As far as I can determine," she said.

"But where are they being beamed?" Sophia asked. "And why?"

"I'm still trying to figure that out. I've done several calculations, but I've come up a little short."

"Why are they playing *these* programs?" I asked.

"That's the funny thing. You probably don't remember the year 1973?"

"Uh, we weren't born yet," Sophia said.

"Well, I was doing my Library Science and Extra-terrestrial Life degree that year. In 1973 the Montreal Canadiens won the Stanley Cup, beating the Chicago

Blackhawks four games to two. Vincent Price, a "horrible" actor – that's a joke – kids, was on Front Page Challenge, and The Friendly Giant was one of the most popular shows for children."

I stared at the hockey game. "But I don't get what's so great about 1973. Why are the aliens stuck in that year?"

"This happened." She pressed a button and all the monitors showed a rocket taking off into space. "It's the launching of Anik 1. Canada's first satellite. These were three of the shows that it help broadcast to all of Canada. Oh, and, accidentally, to the rest of the universe."

"So the aliens watched these shows?" Sophia said.

"Eventually. The shows shot through space to them and they copied them, studied them and looped them. And now they're using the shows against us."

"Do they want to take over Nanaimo? Vancouver Island? The world?" Sophia asked.

Deb shook her head. "I don't think so. At least I would be very surprised. The Denebians were not on the list of ET conquerables."

"Conquerables?" I asked.

"Aliens most likely to conquer us. From what I have been able to find out – and our information on the Denebians is very sketchy – they are the quiet and shy type of alien. So this whole invasion of Nanaimo is out of character for them."

"Well, how do we stop them?" I absently tapped a screen and it came to life flashing the words: *The Real Google*.

"Don't touch that! This is all very sensitive equipment." She paused. "Anyway, we have to find out where the alpha waves are being sent. It would have to be a tall building."

I cogitated hard, my thoughts spinning like a circular saw ready to cut into the truth.

"Archie thinks it's big tall," Archimedes said. "That's where."

For a moment I thought he was just mumbling, then I knew he was right. "You're right, Archie! The Bastion tower," I said. "I even saw antennas on it. I bet that's where the alien is."

Deb tapped the floor with her walking stick. "I think you're right. It makes absolutely perfect sense and it was right there under my nose all the time."

CHAPTER SIXTEEN

STORMING THE TOWER

Deb led us to the door, but stopped there. "I can't go any further," she said. "With my bad leg and all, I won't be any help, but I can give you this." She handed me a slim, white device.

"An MP3 player! Thanks, I can crank up my favourite classical music."

"No, you silly young man. This is a translator. Put it on and you'll be able to understand the words of the aliens."

"Oh," I said. "That makes sense. Where did you get this? Even NASA doesn't have this kind of technology. Or the Canadian Space Agency."

"Librarians invented this so we could communicate with you kids. It's hard to keep track of your 'cool' and 'awesome' words. It just so happens that it translates alien languages too. Anyway, this is very important: if you press the red button, it'll send out a shock wave that'll destroy the surrounding area."

"What?" Sophia and I said at the same time.

"Just kidding!" She laughed. Librarian humour! It takes awhile to get used to it. About two million years or so. "The signal it sends out will be a low electron wave that'll stop any of those segmentoids in their tracks. But it only works once."

"So we better choose wisely when we use it," Sophia said.

"Exactly! I want you two to wear these." She produced two small headsets with mikes and tiny pencil cams. "I'll be able to see through the camera and talk you through the whole mission."

"You make it sound like you're the sergeant," I said.

"I prefer to think of myself as more of a commander-in-chief. Anyway, I think now we should just scout the area. Don't go inside, we have no idea what's waiting there. At the first sign of trouble, I expect you to come directly back here. The bunker under the library is the safest place if a full-fledged invasion erupts."

We nodded, then put on our little headsets, turned on our microphones and began the walk to the Bastion.

"Test, test," Deb said in my ear.

"Test, test," Archimedes answered from my shoulder. "Oh, it works. All systems go. Good luck."

It was a short walk. When we turned onto Gordon Street and saw the white wooden tower of the Bastion, a lump of fear grew in my throat. I swallowed and then my guts began to churn. The Bastion, which had been built as a tower to protect the traders who worked for the Hudson's Bay Company and their families, now looked ominous and frightening to me. To top it off, it was getting cloudy and the sun had decided now was a nice time to play hide and seek in the clouds. Maybe it didn't want to see what was about to happen next.

"Uh, are you feeling what I'm feeling?" I asked Sophia.

"Fear? Fright? Horror?" She tried to smile. "Nope. Not at all. I've moved into complete terror."

"I keep thinking how they knocked out Cheryl just like that. A full-grown sasquatch! If they catch us, we don't really have a chance!"

"Buck up you two!" a voice shouted in my ear. I forgot Deb was monitoring everything. "You don't have to go inside. Just sneak past the perimeter – I'm recording everything you see. Once we have enough footage, we'll make a plan or try to get a message to the mainland."

I breathed in. "Buck up!" Archimedes said. "Buck up right now!" His hearing was obviously good, but even he looked a little frightened.

We looped around, going past the old anchor and getting a good view of the harbour. The only things moving out there were seagulls. Normally there would be all sorts of boating action on the water, even seaplanes landing, but not today.

The Bastion appeared to be deserted. There were still antennas and one satellite dish, but nothing was moving, other than the clouds in the sky. We circled around, this time getting a little closer.

"Do you hear that?" Sophia asked.

I stopped. Listened. A low moaning sound reverberated in the distance, but I couldn't place what direction it was coming from.

"I do hear it. But have no idea what it is."

I looked towards the Bastion and saw that the black front door was open. Inside were shadows, but I thought I could see a shape.

A hairy shape.

"Cheryl!" I said.

"Where?" Sophia asked.

"Where?" Deb said at the same time into my ear.

"Right in the front door of the Bastion. I'm going to try to get closer. You stay here, Sophia."

I crept up, hiding behind the bushes near the Bastion. I peaked around the corner. Cheryl was standing about three feet inside the door, staring out.

"Is she in a trance?" Sophia asked.

"I told you to stay back! You don't follow commands very well."

"I don't follow your commands!"

"The two of you keep it down," Deb said. "I'm trying to see what's going on with Cheryl. Point your heads that way."

We did.

"That noise is getting louder," Sophia whispered.

She was right. It seemed to be coming from all around us. It sounded kind of like OHHHEEEOH and gradually it surrounded us, getting so loud my eardrums rattled. I glanced down towards the harbour.

There were Nanaimotonians of all shapes, ages and sizes trudging towards the Bastion. They had their hands out in front of them and were moving in a wall. It looked like every man, woman and child from Nanaimo was slowly encircling us.

"OHHHHEAHOA," they kept chanting with each slow step. "OOOOOHHHHEEEEEOOOOOA."

"Uh, Deb," I nearly shouted. "We've got mega trouble."

"You should *ccrrzzjk* right now!"

"Pardon?" I asked.

"*Crzyysk! Cfrryly!*" Her signal cut out. It was as though the noise of the Nanaimoite robot zombies was blocking her signal.

"OOOOOHEAAHHHHHHOOOO." They slouched closer. Thousands of feet, thousands of voices, thousands of hands clutching at the air. Postmen, postwomen, policemen, firewomen, teachers, town councillors, senior citizens – they were all there, like a giant Nanaimo amoeba.

"They may be dangerous," I said.

"The only safe place is the Bastion," Sophia said.

"You're right."

And without a second thought we ran straight for the front door of the Bastion.

CHAPTER SEVENTEEN

OUT OF THE FRYING PAN INTO THE BASTION

With each thudding step I heard a voice in my head saying, "Bad move!" Then it dawned on me that it was Archimedes squawking, "Bad move! Archie thinks this is a bad move!"

Was he right? Should we stop and face the robotified zombies? But what if they caught us and force-fed Nanaimo bars to us? We'd become just like them.

I couldn't make up my mind. Imagine, a mind as smart as mine and I couldn't get it to analyze what was the best course of action. My feet were doing my thinking for me, because I was already on the steps leading up to the Bastion door. Sophia was right beside me.

"Archie's not going there!" Archimedes screeched, and at the last minute he launched himself off my shoulder and into the air. "Don't go!"

Sophia and I smacked the door the rest of the way open. The light fell on Cheryl who was hung in the air like a prize catch, her arms manacled and eyes closed. Her head sagged down. She was definitely out for the count.

I caught my breath, my ears were buzzing. I was obviously completely out of shape. I glanced back out the door. All of the zombies were in a line circling around the Bastion. They had stopped and were staring up with wide, hypnotized eyes, still murmuring, "ooooowwwahhhooo."

I saw my mom and dad and my knees nearly gave out. They looked so…so…1970s! It was terrible. What if they stayed that way forever? They didn't move their eyes from staring at the top of the Bastion.

"There are my parents!" Sophia said. I saw them, dressed similarly to my parents, that dull look in their eyes. "It's awful! So awful."

I put my hand on her shoulder. "We'll save them. I know we will." But Sophia still looked shocked and sad and I thought the best thing to get her focussed again would be to close the door, so I pushed it shut.

The buzzing in my ears grew louder.

Waiting behind the door was a swarm of the robot bees. Their multi-faceted eyes stared at us. Their big metallic abdomens glistened as needles poked out, dripping with what I could only assume was bee-sting venom.

I reached for the neutralizer button on the translator. One bee zipped out of the formation and stabbed its needle right into my arm. I felt a sharp pain and my left arm froze from the elbow down.

"YYYEOWWCH!" I screamed. "I can't move my arm."

The swarm hovered menacingly. "Don't move at all!" Sophia whispered. "They seem to react to motion."

I blinked. Slowly. I didn't want them going for my eyes.

"Can you hear us, Deb?" I whispered into my mike. "Deb? What do we do?"

There was no answer.

"Any plans?" I asked Sophia. "I can't touch the neutralizer."

She slipped off her shoe and kicked it towards the wall. Twenty bees followed, stinging it before it hit the ground. At that same moment she jumped at me, reached out and hit the neutralizer button. The remaining bees dived for her.

The device glowed green and made a PFFFSTZZT sound. All the bees suddenly stopped flapping their wings and thudded to the floor like falling metal bullets.

"It worked!" I said. "It worked!"

"Yeah, but now we won't be able to use it again."

I shrugged. "There wasn't anything else we could do. Good thinking on your part."

We went over to check on Cheryl. She was hanging up in the middle of the room like an old forgotten furry coat. Her eyes were shut tight and she snored a little. Two metallic manacles clung to her wrists and they glowed a light blue colour. It was all that held her – somehow those devices were making her levitate in one place.

"Cheryl," I said. "Wake up. Cheryl."

She didn't budge. Sophia reached out and pinched her toe. Still no budging. I pulled on her arm then flipped one eyelid up. Her eye was rolled back in its socket. "There's no one home."

The "UHHHWOWAAS" were getting louder outside and for the first time I heard a noise upstairs. I looked out the window again. My parents were still standing there like zombies. I'd sometimes thought they were mindless but now it was true. My mom was someone who was hard to keep up with, always talking and walking fast. And Dad, he was a quick thinker, always ready with a joke. Now neither of them moved with any speed, they just stood staring up at the top floor of the Bastion.

It made me angry. I saw red. Who would dare to do this to my parents? To Sophia's parents? To all the Nanaimoiters. What had we ever done to anyone else?

I looked around for a weapon. The shelves had all sorts of stuff from trader's days: blankets, sacks of flour, salt, buttons. But I needed an ax. I needed to stop this whole attack.

I let out a deep breath. Sucked in some air. Then let out another deep breath. I was getting madder.

"That's your 'anger' breath," Sophia said.

I nodded. "I've had enough! I'm giving these aliens a piece of my mind!"

I stomped away from her and up the old stairs to the second floor. My mind had stopped. I wasn't thinking anymore.

"Wait!" Sophia said. "What are you doing, Gordon?"

There was more museum stuff on the second floor. Light came in from the old windows, one wooden shutter was slightly open. Two cannons sat there and I wondered if I could load them up and shoot holes in the ceiling. Maybe the noise would wake up all the Nanaimotonians outside. The walls were all rough-hewn logs and there was a display of old muskets. I yanked at them, but they wouldn't come out of the display.

I didn't need a gun. I'd use my bare hands if I had to. I marched to the steep set of stairs and started to climb.

There came a tugging on my pant leg. "You're being crazy! You don't have a plan. You always have a plan!"

"They can't have Nanaimo!" I declared. "It's my town!"

"Our town," Sophia said.

With each step a humming grew louder and louder. I burst onto the third floor, where the old traders would hold meetings. Today, it would be a meeting between human and alien.

CHAPTER EIGHTEEN

CONTACT AND THEN MORE CONTACT

The shutters were all closed, but the room glowed green. And it was hot and humid, as though I was walking into a deep, dark jungle. The floor, oddly enough, looked as though it had been carefully polished. Sophia was one step behind me.

The third floor was the largest of the three – it was built in a saucer shape. I looked around, finding that my anger was slipping away and I was beginning to use my brain again.

I thought things like: *What am I gonna do if it attacks me? Does it have a ray gun? Why am I standing here facing an alien that has enough power to take over the whole town?* My knees began to quake.

There was an assembly line in the corner – a square glass-doored machine that opened and a pan of Nanaimo bars came out. Nano ants scurried over, carried it through what looked to be a portal into nothingness, and disappeared. It must be a transporter. So that's how they got from one part of the town to another.

A second later, the door opened, and another pan of bars was ready. Another group of ants carried it towards the portal. Where the Nanaimo bars were coming from, I didn't know. They just materialized out of nowhere.

Several theories leapt to my brain at once. Perhaps they were being made in another dimension, proof that the string theory was correct. It could even be the tenth dimension! Or they came from a factory on Mars. I didn't have time to theorize, I needed to act.

On the other wall was a bank of tiny TVs each playing a show from the seventies. The aliens must be broadcasting from here. All along the ceiling were blue and green glowing wires that looked like veins.

"The wires appear to lead up into the antennas outside," Sophia said.

"Good observation," I whispered. "Can you see an alien?"

She was slowly looking around. "No. Maybe they're gone."

I took another step. I could still hear the AWOOOGHA of the people outside. In fact it seemed to be getting louder. The top of the tower pulsed with the sound. The hairs on my arms began to stand straight up. I trudged ahead, ready for anything. The numbness in my arm was finally starting to go away, but there was still a sharp pain where the robot bee had stung me.

When I reached the centre of the room, I stopped. "There's no one here," I said. "The aliens have vanished."

Sophia nodded. "Look at the wires. They glow each time the crowd makes a noise."

"You're right! And all the energy seems to be going into this glowing ball right here." I pointed at the ceiling. The spinning blue-green ball was getting larger. "It's like it's gathering up something from the people outside."

"Alpha waves!" we both said at the same time.

I took a step closer to the ball. It was growing brighter and seemed to be making a humming noise. "Yes, all of Nanaimo's alpha waves are being stored here. But for what? It's like a giant battery. Or energy source."

"It must be sucking all the IQ out of our parents," Sophia said.

"That's the last straw! My parents need their IQs! We have to shut this machine down."

I looked around for a switch. There was an odd machine that had several spinning, glowing gyroscopes.

The blue and green wires were attached to it. I took a step, the boards creaking beneath my feet.

"Gordon!"

A blue-green blur streaked through the air and struck my right shoulder. My whole arm went numb. Something was scrabbling around on my back, but before I could turn I felt a pinprick of pain on my neck and my whole spine froze. A microsecond later, another stabbing pain froze my left arm. I was a Gordon Whillickers statue.

"Mean humans! Mean humans! You have dirt on your shoes!"

I couldn't move. Sophia screamed behind me and I could only imagine she was going through the same thing. But maybe she saw who or what was attacking us. "Mean earthling! Didn't even wash behind your ears. That's very unclean."

Sophia suddenly stopped yelling. "Sophia," I said. "Are you all right?"

I wished I could turn my head or move to help her. But I was frozen in place. "Sophia, say something."

All I heard was a mumbled, *"mytungz frossen."*

"What? Oh, your tongue is frozen."

Then the alien hopped up on the display in the middle of the room. He wasn't much bigger than a frog. His skin was green. His large eyes stared at us. He was standing on two long legs, his green hands sprouting short tentacles that were wrapped around a glowing pin. I assume that was what he had used to freeze us. He was probably small because of heavier gravity on his home world.

"You look like a frog."

"Thank you. Why do I understand your words?" he asked.

I still had the earbuds in from the translator. "I'm wearing a translator."

"Oh. Hmm. Well, you have been very persistent. Overly persistent, in fact. I am *Istinstongriongoandinddingoron*, but you can call me Ronald. Excuse me, I must vacuum up this dustball." He reached down and pulled a miniature vacuum cleaner from the desk. He turned it on and went to work, then began cleaning the floor where we had walked.

"Dirty shoes," he said. "All things must be neat. All things clean and in order." He sounded like my parents. Then at once I realized that *he* had turned them all into neat freaks. "I must not bring any germs home," he said.

"Home?" I echoed. "Are you going home?"

Ron jumped back up to the middle of the table and flicked off the vacuum. "I must. And I shall gently and ever so kindly suck out your brains before I go. Cleanly, of course."

"What?" I desperately wished I could move.

The alien smiled, showing white, sharp teeth. He definitely wasn't a frog. "I just made a joke. No, fear not, earthling child. I make fun."

"What are you doing to my parents? To all the Nanaimotorians?"

"I am borrowing their brainwaves to open a portal in time and space so that I can return to my home planet. Isn't that obvious?" Ronald scratched his alien forehead. "It's obvious to me."

"Borrowing?"

"Well, they won't get them back, sadly. Once this is done. Brains shall be, oh, how do you humans say it, fried."

"You're going to fry our parents' brains?"

"You can't!" Sophia said. "No!" Good! She could speak again.

"I'm afraid it's my only way home. I realize that this is a troublesome thing for you, but it's a small sacrifice, really. You humans rarely use your brains."

"But it's wrong," I argued. "Don't you have a code of some sort, or a directive? You shouldn't interfere with the human race, right?"

"Codes! Directives! They're all so confusing and tiresome. We try not to interfere, most of the time. But I have been trapped here for too many revolutions around your sun. I got sucked through the wrong vortex. I thought I was going on vacation but I was stuck here instead. Your planet is extremely boring. I must go home. I miss my moms."

"Moms?"

"Yes, all Denebians are born of two mothers. Don't they educate you here?"

"But you can't fry our parents brains," I said. "We wouldn't fry *your* moms' brains."

Ronald stopped to think. He put a finger to his chin. "First, I should explain, my moms don't have brains, they have cerebral sacs in their stomachs. But I do see your point. Would you humans fry their cerebral sacs? Hmmm. Maybe I should try and find another plan."

"Yes, we could help you."

Ronald let out a high, squealing laugh. "Help? From a human? You don't even have cerebral sacs. No, no, no, I'm afraid I must proceed. If I tried to find another plan, it might take many of your years. I have changed my mind once again. This plan is much easier. Plus, remember the frogs."

"The frogs! What frogs?"

"I feel very close to the frogs on this planet. They are the highest life form here. And you're poisoning them all with your pesticides and toxic chemicals. Nope, I'm afraid we'll have to follow my plan."

He rubbed his tentacled fingers together. "AHHH. All is ready, the IQ readings are at their peak." He leapt over to a switch in the wall. "I am afraid I must do this. I apologize for any discomfort it causes you. As I said, I will be wiping your brains clean too."

"You can't have our brains!" I tried to move but couldn't budge a millimetre.

"No!" Sophia cried out. "I like my brain!"

"Ah, but it must be done. Goodbye to you. Enjoy your somnambulant state. It will be very pleasant and peaceful."

He reached for the switch and pulled it halfway up. The room began to hum and buzz and the veins of glowing power pulsed. I felt my brain pulse too, as though my very thoughts were being sucked up into the centre of the dome.

"Darn switch!" Ronald said, his green tentacles tugging on it. "I should have oiled it. Ah, there it goes."

He pulled it three quarters of the way up. Now my skull was throbbing, the noise outside of every Nanaimoinian was growing louder. I imagined all of their alpha waves being sucked out of their heads. Just near the centre of the room a glowing circle was being formed.

Ronald clicked the switch all the way up and the room began to vibrate and a SHWEEERETTEEEE sound surrounded us. It was the sound of a hole being punched in the fabric of the universe.

"There it is!" Ronald said, clapping his tentacled hands in glee. "A door home. No more earth gravity, no more carbon monoxide, no more Oprah!"

He took a step towards the centre of the room.

I could wiggle a finger. I was surprised that I could move very slightly. It did seem like my brain was about to explode.

"So hard to think," Sophia said. "We must do something."

I could wiggle two fingers but not much else. I would never get out in time.

Then suddenly, without warning, the shutter banged open as though a cannonball had hit it and sunlight flooded the room.

CHAPTER NINETEEN

AMAZING AERIAL MANOEUVRES

Ronald looked over in time to see a comet of feathers and beak – Archimedes – slam into him. All was a blur as the two tussled. Archimedes yelled, "You are a bad extraterrestrial! Real Bad!" Then with a great swoop of his grey wings, he grabbed Ronald by the shoulders and carried him out the window, his claws digging into the alien's shoulder.

He held him above the ground, swooping back and forth next to the window. "Archie might drop you!" he said teasing.

"Don't! Stupid ornithop! Don't drop me. And don't eat me."

I could move my feet now and I chugged ahead, through the noise. The whirring in my brain and in the room grew louder.

Ronald was shaking his limbs and his tentacles, trying to grab at Archimedes.

With my last bit of strength I lurched ahead. My brain was going blank. I blinked and saw only darkness. Then I was in the room again. Were my memories being erased? I tipped like a statue, falling forward to hit the switch back down.

Click! I thought I heard, then I hit my head on the wall and fell to the floor. A few seconds or years passed, then I was able to move my arm. Someone was tugging on my arms.

"Get up, Gordon," Sophia said.

She pulled me up. The space portal went PFFFZZT and closed with what I could only describe as a gaseous sound. Archimedes was still flapping his wings, circling outside the window. The Denebian looked scared, and Archimedes looked tired.

"You wrecked it all!" Ronald shouted.

Below them, watching like crazy, was every Nanaimoite. They had stopped their moaning and were staring up. I spotted Mom and Dad, and they appeared confused.

"Bring him in here," I said.

Archimedes swooped in and dropped Ronald in my hand. He didn't seem to have any weapons.

"Foolish human being! Now I will never get home."

"I'm sorry. But we couldn't let you destroy Nanaimo. Or at least all the brains in Nanaimo."

"What are we going to do with him?" Sophia asked.

"Let me handle that."

I turned. Cheryl had come up the stairs. She moved quietly for someone so large. "Hello, Denebian."

"You! You were trying to stop my plans!"

"There is another way home," Cheryl said. She put out her hand and I plopped the alien into it. She closed her hands, leaving only Ronald's head in the open.

"I can get you home. All you had to do was ask. I've got the technology."

"You do?" I asked.

"Yes," she said. "Sasquatches have all the technology. We just choose not to use it. Watch tonight and you'll see a light show from the island."

"How would you get me home?" Ronald asked. "Listen, sasquatch – I have friends. Important friends."

"Let's just say its a subparticle accelerator machine. With a few anti-grav jets for good measure."

"Anti-grav jets. Ahhh, that does sound intriguing." He seemed happy. "You're still bad humans," he said, looking at us. "You should wash behind your ears."

"Well, I hope we're nicer than you when we visit *your* planet."

"Hmmmph. Lower life forms. You get so cheeky sometimes. You haven't heard the last of Ronald." Cheryl gave him a bit of a squeeze. "On second thought, you probably have."

Cheryl put her other hand on my shoulder, still keeping a tight grip on Ronald. "I really liked working with you," she said.

"Yeah, me too," I added. "Will we see you again? Or will you become a legend?"

Cheryl laughed. I realized that it was a beautiful sound. "Oh, we'll meet again, my friends."

"Good," Sophia said and she gave Cheryl a hug. "We need more friends like you."

"Yes, we need big smart friends," Archie added.

That got another laugh out of Cheryl. Then, with alien in hand, she walked over to the steps.

"How are you getting out of here?" I asked. "You don't want all the people to see you, do you?"

She shook her head. "There's a tunnel in the basement of the Bastion. It comes out on Protection Island. There's a tunnel everywhere in Nanaimo. You just have to be trained to see them."

Then she was gone.

"Well," Sophia said. "Should we go downstairs?"

I nodded.

CHAPTER TWENTY

THE END OF THE BEGINNING

We explained to the crowd that it was a special holiday and that's why the whole city was standing in front of the Bastion. No one believed us or seemed to understand, but once Debbie the librarian came out and told everyone the same thing, they all nodded their heads. They just couldn't believe it from two kids.

Mom and Dad had returned to normal. I could tell because the first thing Mom said was, "Gordon, get that MP3 player out of your ears. It'll rot your brain." I gave them both a hug, then Sophia and I herded our parents back to the Volvo.

"How did the car get here?" Dad asked.

"Uh, the librarians parked it there," I said.

That seemed to settle him down, but once we got nearer he asked, "How did it get so many tiny dents?"

"Hail," I answered, secretly flicking a dead metallic ant off the windshield wiper. "It was a very sudden hailstorm. It'll be in the front page of the paper tomorrow, I'm sure."

"I'm starving," Mom said. "We should get going, dear. We can talk about the weather later."

Dad scratched his head. "How did I get so much gel in my hair?"

Mom touched her own hair. "And why do I have curlers?"

"I think it will all make sense after we eat," I said. That seemed to satisfy them.

After dropping Sophia and her parents off, the first thing we did was cook hot dogs. I ate four. I had burned a lot of energy that last few hours.

Then my parents went straight to bed. I was tired too, so I went to my room and wrote a few notes about everything that had happened.

Sophia climbed up through the window. "My parents are already in bed," she said. "They were exhausted. But they appear to be normal. They said they'd had nightmares about Nanaimo bars."

"Mine seem normal too," I said.

I shook her hand.

"What was that for?"

"Good job."

Then came an amazingly loud roaring, like fireworks going off. At first I thought it was something going wrong at the docks, an explosion, maybe, but it grew louder and louder. Maybe a jet was making a sonic boom. Sophia and I dashed out to the backyard and looked up at the sky. At first we didn't see anything, then a flaming star shot into the sky. It seemed to have taken off from Newcastle Island.

"It looks like fireworks," Sophia said.

"Well, Ronald's going home," I said. "Goodbye. I'll be happy not to meet another alien for awhile."

We watched the sky for a minute or two, then I patted Sophia on the back. "We did a good job," I said. "And no one will ever know."

"Except Cheryl and the librarian."

"What do we do next?" I asked.

"Well, did I tell you I've been taking scuba diving lessons?"

"No. Why?"

"Oh, I always wondered if Ogopogo is real. I mean sasquatches are real. Maybe she is too."

"Ogopogo is a she?" I asked.

"Well, we won't know until we find her."

"Archie thinks you're crazy!" Archimedes said. "Very Crazy!"

I laughed. Then my brilliant mind began to work on a plan. "We might need a submarine."

I took a deep breath. "Next summer," I said. "We'll look then. We're gonna take the rest of this summer off."

ACKNOWLEDGEMENTS

My thanks to Barbara Sapergia, Mary Reid and all my relatives and friends who put up with my visits to the island.

ABOUT THE AUTHOR

Arthur Slade is one of Canada's best-known and most respected writers of fiction for young readers. His novel *Dust*, set in Depression-era Saskatchewan, won the Governor General's Award for Children's Literature, the Mr. Christie Book Award, and the Saskatchewan Book Award for Children's Literature; it was also nominated for a prestigious American award, the Edgar, for mystery writing.

His other books include *Tribes, Draugr, The Loki Wolf,* and *The Haunting of Drang Island.*

In 2002, Coteau Books launched Art's exciting and entertaining new series, *Canadian Chills.* The first title, *Return of the Grudstone Ghosts,* won the Diamond Willow Award of the Saskatchewan Young Readers Choice Awards in 2004, the same year the second in the series, *Ghost Hotel,* was launched.

Arthur Slade was raised on a ranch in Saskatchewan's Cypress Hills and now lives in Saskatoon.

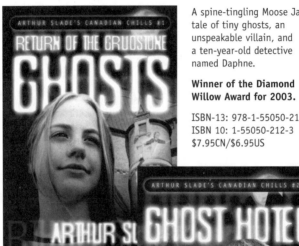

MEMBER OF SCABRINI GROUP

Québec, Canada
2007